Also by Kate Banks

Friends of the Heart / Amici del Cuore
Walk Softly, Rachel
Dillon Dillon
Howie Bowles and Uncle Sam
Howie Bowles, Secret Agent

Picture Books
Fox
Max's Words
The Great Blue House
The Cat Who Walked Across France
Mama's Coming Home
Close Your Eyes
The Turtle and the Hippopotamus
A Gift from the Sea
The Night Worker
The Bird, the Monkey, and the Snake in the Jungle
And If the Moon Could Talk
Baboon
Spider Spider

Lenny's Space

Kate Banks
Lenny's Space

FRANCES FOSTER BOOKS
FARRAR, STRAUS AND GIROUX
NEW YORK

www.fsgkidsbooks.com

Library of Congress Cataloging-in-Publication Data
Banks, Kate, date.
    Lenny's space / Kate Banks.— 1st ed.
        p.   cm.
    Summary: Nine-year-old Lenny gets in trouble and has no friends because
he cannot control himself in school and his interests are not like those of his
classmates, until he starts visiting Muriel, a counselor, and meets Van, a boy his
age who has leukemia.
    ISBN-13: 978-0-374-34575-4
    ISBN-10: 0-374-34575-9
    [1. Single-parent families—Fiction.   2. Counselors—Fiction.   3. Friendship—
Fiction.   4. Schools—Fiction.   5. Leukemia—Fiction.]   I. Title.

PZ7.B22594Le 2007
[Fic]—dc22

                                                                    2006037384

For Muriel ♥

Lenny's Space

1

Lenny Brewster looked at the three wobbly stacks of Cheerios he'd piled up on the table in front of him. "How do you think they cook these things?" he asked.

"I have no idea," said his mother. She swooped down and whisked the plates from the table. "You're going to be late for school," she added. She was wearing a pair of white cotton wrist-length gloves. Lenny thought they made her look like a waitress.

"Don't forget these," said Lenny, passing her the eggcups filled with flesh-colored shells.

"Thanks," said his mother.

Lenny's mother was a hand model. That's why she wore gloves. She wore them all the time. And she had an entire collection, in every imaginable color. She had to protect her hands so that they'd always be perfect. No cuts or scrapes, no broken nails, no age spots or wrinkles.

Lenny's mother didn't mind the gloves. She'd gotten used to them. To her they were like a second skin, another defense against life's blows. Lenny, on the other hand, hated those gloves. To him they were like a steel barrier, which spoiled one of the most basic pleasures of any child—holding his mother's hand.

Lenny watched his mother load the dishwasher in record time. When she whizzed around the house engaging appliances she was like one herself, fast and efficient.

"Do you have a battery or something?" Lenny asked.

"A battery?" asked his mother.

"A battery that makes you go so fast," said Lenny.

Lenny's mother gave him a puzzled look. Then she pushed buttons on the washing machine and the dishwasher. She set everything on the delayed program so that the commotion wouldn't begin until they'd left. Lenny sighed wistfully, realizing he would again miss the humming, whirring symphony of appliances that testified to the ingenuity of science. Lenny loved science. He loved the notion that everything had a special way of working. Someday he wanted to invent something, though he didn't yet know what.

Lenny's mother fed the fish, sprinkling a few flakes of food into the tank on the countertop. There were four of them. Lenny had named them One Fish, Two Fish, Red Fish, Blue Fish after a book that he'd had when he was five. It didn't matter that Red Fish was more of an orange color and Blue Fish purple. Lenny had loved that book, and his fish reminded him of it.

Lenny sniffed the flakes of food. "That stuff smells like dead fish," he said. "Do you think they feed live fish dead fish?"

"Probably," said his mother. She stuffed his books, which were staggered across the table like playing cards, into his book bag. Then she leaned down into Lenny's face.

"You need to hurry up," she said.

Lenny went back to his piles of Cheerios. He inhaled deeply in preparation for the final blow. Then he exhaled, sending the three towers of cereal into the air like a summer storm. Most landed on the floor. A few ended up in Lenny's mother's hair.

Lenny's mother had a policy of counting to five before raising her voice.

"One, two, three, four, five," she said. "Grow up, Lenny, and act your age!"

Lenny was nine going on ten. But his mother clasped him by the hand and marched him from the table to the front door as she would a three-year-old.

"They must be full of air," said Lenny, still focused on the Cheerios, wondering about their composition. He reminded himself to check the back of the box when he got home from school.

Lenny's mother handed him his jacket and his book bag. "Tie your sneakers, Lenny," she said.

Lenny leaned over. He wrapped the laces, which were

too long, around his ankles and secured them like Cleopatra's sandals. He'd seen a picture of them when they'd studied Egypt at school. Lenny admired his feet as he followed his mother to the car. His mother looked down but didn't comment.

Lenny climbed into the backseat of the car. "What's for dinner?" he asked.

"You just had breakfast," said his mother. She whipped around a corner—a little too fast.

"You're going to get a speeding ticket," said Lenny.

"Let's hope not," said his mother.

Then she pulled up in front of the school, inches from the curb. Lenny couldn't help but admire her precision.

"I bet you could have been a race car driver," said Lenny.

"Thanks, Lenny," said his mother.

Lenny climbed out of the car and walked toward the school, which loomed large before him. His mother had gotten out of the car, too.

"Lenny!" she cried. "Haven't you forgotten something?"

Lenny turned and ran back. His mother reached into the backseat. As she leaned over, Lenny gave her a quick kiss. She handed Lenny his book bag with her white-gloved hands. Then she crouched down to retie his sneakers. Lenny could have done it himself, but he let his mother do it for him.

Lenny watched his mother get back into the car. She paused for a moment before starting the engine, as if to recharge her battery. Then she pulled away from the curb. She lifted a hand—a white-gloved hand—and waved to Lenny.

Lenny waved back. He tried without success to manage a smile. He could relate to the battery but not to the white-gloved hands.

2

Lenny stood in line waiting for school to begin. Some boys in front of him were trying to guess how many seconds before the bell rang.

"At least one hundred and twenty seconds," thought Lenny, but he didn't say anything. Just in case he was wrong. Being wrong was like losing. And Lenny hated to lose. It filled him with a crushing sense of defeat, a feeling of being worthless.

When the bell finally did ring, Lenny didn't hear it. He was too intent on drawing a small tattoo on the back of his wrist. Lenny had seen a flying dinosaur just that morning on television and didn't want to lose the image. He'd spent a good deal of time pondering whether or not to use indelible ink. He wondered if the animal would get bigger as his arm grew. In the end, he'd decided to use a regular pen. He wasn't sure he wanted an extinct creature on his wrist for the rest of his life.

———

Lenny was pulled along in the current of boys and girls pushing and shoving to get to their classrooms. He sat down at his desk. His fourth-grade teacher, Ms. Schillinger, came around to collect the math homework. Lenny had done all of the problems. Then he'd illustrated them because he thought things looked better with pictures—bright, colorful ones.

"Do you like them?" asked Lenny.

"Wonderful, Leonard," said Ms. Schillinger, rolling her eyes. She had a habit of calling Lenny Leonard. He'd reminded her on several occasions that this was not his name. He was just Lenny. But she kept forgetting.

Ms. Schillinger threw Lenny one of her looks of exasperation that she reserved solely for him. Lots of special looks were reserved for Lenny at school. Lenny wondered if she might send him into another classroom or to Mr. Ourcival, the principal. Maybe she'd even send him to another school.

"Who cares," thought Lenny, picking up a sheet of paper and thinking about what he might do with it. For Lenny all paper became projectiles, all pencils, pens, and erasers playthings.

"Feel free to put the pictures on the wall, Ms. Schillinger," said Lenny. He mispronounced her name, saying it with a soft "g." It was his way of settling the score for her calling him Leonard. Besides, Lenny liked the sound of "Schillinger" with a soft "g." It reminded him of the word "cylinder." Lenny loved cylinders of all types—engines, telescopes, projectiles, pea-shooting guns.

"This isn't first grade, Leonard," said Ms. Schillinger.

"I could do a bunch of pictures," said Lenny. "And you could paper the entire room."

Ms. Schillinger didn't comment.

Lenny shoved his hands under his knees and swung his legs back and forth under his chair. It made him feel good. Then he leaned back and set to work with his pencil sharpener, a small razor encapsulated in a sea green plastic cylinder that collected the shavings if you wished. Lenny did not wish. Therefore he removed the cylinder. He stuck the pencil into the razor and turned it slowly. He hoped to carve one long coil like when you peeled an entire apple and got one unbroken length of skin. Lenny carefully extracted the shaving and held it up proudly. "Look!" he cried.

Ms. Schillinger ignored Lenny. That was her way of dealing with him. Everyone had a different way of dealing with Lenny—his mother, his teacher, the other kids. The principal, Mr. Ourcival, had had several man-to-man talks with Lenny. He'd stood before Lenny and practically threatened him with a punishment if he didn't start behaving as a boy his age should. Mr. Ourcival was a firm believer in punishments. And he doled them out like candy. Lenny didn't mind. He could usually turn them into some playful activity. This sent Mr. Ourcival into paroxysms of frustration that caused his acid reflux to act up. The truth was that Mr. Ourcival didn't deal with frustration very well. Not much better than Lenny.

Lenny didn't seem to grasp the notion that there was a time and place for things. Very often he just said whatever popped into his head.

"You're disturbing the class, Leonard," Ms. Schillinger would often remind him.

"Sorry," said Lenny, looking around and realizing that he was not the only one in the room. He was genuinely repentant. Lenny was mostly selfish, but there were occasions when he exhibited a generous spontaneity that was childlike and winning, like when the first snowflake of the year fell.

"Hey, look!" he cried, hopping out of his seat. "Snow!"

For a moment, the class, pupils and teacher alike, was caught in the wonder of that first snowflake. Lenny also had an endearing way of insulting people and then feeling hurt. In fact, Lenny had many endearing qualities. His joy at certain things was contagious. At the close of the day, other kids would be moaning, waiting for the bell.

Lenny would be working away, and when it rang he'd pop out of his chair like a jack-in-the-box. "I guess it's time to go," he'd say brightly. "See you later, Ms. Schillinger."

Lenny was actually a brilliant student. For him schoolwork was like a game. His teachers had considered moving him ahead a grade, or putting him in a gifted class, partially to get rid of him. But in the end they always ended up admitting that his emotional development was so far behind that it would be disastrous to move him.

Unbeknownst to Lenny, he was the topic of many closed-door meetings and discussions. He was the cause of several teacher and student absences, and numerous purchases of Rolaids on the part of Mr. Ourcival.

The result was that Lenny got passed around like a hot potato—to the principal, to the librarian, and back to his teacher. And it might have gone on like that had it not been for Muriel.

3

Lenny opened the small sheet of notepaper folded and stuffed into a pinkish-colored envelope. It reminded him of a birthday invitation, which he never got because no one wanted Lenny at a party.

On the paper was a message inviting Lenny to stop by room 123 at break time after lunch. The paper was signed by someone named Muriel.

"Who's this Muriel person?" Lenny asked out loud. Then he vaguely remembered his mother mentioning a meeting with someone at school. She'd said that Lenny would be meeting this person, too. "This must be her," said Lenny to himself.

• • •

Lenny skipped sideways down the hallway, reeling off the room numbers in a loud voice.

"One twenty-one, one twenty-two, one twenty-three,"

he said. Then he stopped. The door to room 123 was ajar. Lenny peeked in.

"Are you Leonard?" a lady asked.

Lenny guessed that the lady must be Muriel.

"Come in," she said.

"I'm Lenny, not Leonard," said Lenny.

"Okay," said Muriel. "I can remember that."

"I'm glad someone can," said Lenny.

He sat down in the chair across from Muriel. It was a revolving chair with a padded fabric back and seat. Moreover, it was a twin to the chair in which Muriel was sitting. That made Lenny feel good. Lenny paid a lot of attention to chairs. Mr. Ourcival sat in nothing short of a throne in the principal's office. His chair was enormous, with thick padded leather and a spring coil that allowed him to lean back, to the left, or to the right. Mr. Ourcival looked foreboding in that chair, especially when Lenny faced him from his vantage point: a small wooden chair with broken slats.

"My name is Muriel," said the lady.

"Hi, Muriel," said Lenny.

The first thing Lenny noticed about Muriel was her sky blue cardigan sweater, which had a row of big, round buttons, each with three holes. Lenny liked those. He tilted his head and looked down at her shoes. Lenny was convinced that shoes said a lot about a person. Ms. Schillinger wore dull brown walking shoes. Mr. Ourcival wore large black pointy-toed shoes. Lenny himself wore blue-and-white sneakers with little flashing lights built into the soles.

Muriel's shoes were red with an alligator-like texture. But they had soft, rounded toes and flat heels. Lenny instantly liked them. On the whole, he liked Muriel. The color of her nails, which matched one of the more exotic colors in his collection of Magic Markers. Her glasses, with their longish rectangular frames. She was tall and thin, like a pretzel stick, and Lenny smiled when he thought of this. It made him hungry.

"I'm hungry," said Lenny.

Muriel reached into her bag—green canvas with blue alligators swimming on the outside—and pulled out a packet of crackers. She handed them to Lenny. Then she got right to the point.

"I'm here to help you, Lenny," said Muriel.

"Oh, I can do it myself," said Lenny.

He quickly busied himself with the task of opening the crackers. Pulling apart the cellophane and letting the air out like a giant fart. He grinned knowingly. Muriel grinned back. Lenny began eating. It didn't occur to him to offer Muriel one.

"How old are you, Lenny?" Muriel asked.

"Nine and a half," said Lenny. "My birthday's in July. When's yours?"

"February," said Muriel.

"It's not the twenty-ninth, is it?" said Lenny.

"No," said Muriel.

"Because if it was," said Lenny, "you'd only have a birthday every four years."

"I'm not sure I'd like that," said Muriel.

"I would," said Lenny.

Lenny popped out of his chair and walked over to Muriel's bookshelves. They were lined with all kinds of objects. A row of small seashells. Another of figurines. Some colored blocks. Balls and marbles in varying sizes. Pinecones. Rocks and crystals. It was nice to see an adult with so many playthings.

"You're lucky," said Lenny. "They let you bring toys to school."

"They're not really toys," said Muriel. "I use them when I work."

"What do you do?" asked Lenny.

"I work with children," said Muriel. "I talk to them and try to help them figure out what's going on in their worlds. Sometimes we use the toys on that shelf."

"Oh," said Lenny. "Does that mean I get to play with those things?"

"If you'd like," said Muriel.

Lenny grabbed a SuperBall and tossed it into the air. It bounced off the ceiling and ricocheted across the room.

"What do you like to do, Lenny?" asked Muriel.

"I like to fix things," said Lenny. "And I'm good at it. Got anything that needs fixing?"

Muriel reached inside the desk behind her for a pen.

"As a matter of fact, I do," she said. "I can't seem to get this pen to work."

Lenny took the pen and sat down. He unscrewed it.

"It's the spring," he said. "It's in upside down."

Lenny emptied out the spring and jammed it back into the pen the other way around.

"See?" he said.

"Thank you, Lenny," said Muriel.

She scribbled some small circles on a notepad with the pen.

"What do you like to play, Lenny?" she asked.

"I like games," said Lenny. "And I like to make things."

"Would you like to play something now?" asked Muriel.

"Sure," said Lenny.

Muriel got up and cleared a space on a bookshelf. Then she took a label and wrote on it with the pen that Lenny had fixed: LENNY'S SPACE. She stuck the label to the floor of the bookshelf.

"From now on, this is going to be your space, Lenny," she said. "So let's start by putting something here that'll make us think of you. You can choose from any of those objects on the shelf."

Lenny walked over to the shelf. He picked up a Mexican jumping bean.

"This is like me," he said. "Everyone says I can't sit still."

"Okay," said Muriel.

Lenny put the bean in the middle of his space. He clapped his hands and watched it jump. The harder he clapped, the higher it jumped.

"You clap, Muriel, and see how high I can jump," said Lenny.

Muriel clapped and Lenny jumped.

"Do you like to jump, Lenny?" asked Muriel.

"Yup," said Lenny. He jumped to the door and back again.

"That was a lot of jumping," said Muriel. "Do you feel better now?"

"Yup," said Lenny. He was all out of breath. "I feel good," he said.

Lenny looked at the jumping bean, which was now still.

"Do you want to add anything else to your space, Lenny?" asked Muriel.

Lenny paused. He couldn't really decide. At last he said, "No."

"Okay," said Muriel. "Maybe another time."

"Are you going to give me any homework?" asked Lenny.

"Would you like some?" asked Muriel.

"Sure," said Lenny. "If it's something to play."

"Let's see," said Muriel. "I bet you can dress yourself."

"Of course I can," said Lenny. "But sometimes I let my mother tie my shoes and close my buttons. She likes doing it."

"Do you like that?" asked Muriel.

Lenny thought for a moment. "Not really," he said.

"Who chooses your clothes?" asked Muriel.

"My mother does that part," said Lenny.

"Okay," said Muriel. "Now I want you to do that part. You choose what you want to wear."

"Can I choose anything?" said Lenny. He looked surprised.

"Anything," said Muriel. "But I want you to be responsible for the buttons, snaps, and laces. No help from anyone."

"Okay," said Lenny. "This sounds fun."

4

Lenny delved into his drawer. He was looking for his favorite pair of camping shorts, the ones with seven pockets and a key chain holder attached to a belt loop. They were at the bottom along with his other summer clothes. Lenny pulled them out, causing a small landslide in the drawer. He left the mound of bunched-up clothes for his mother to straighten out.

Lenny put on the shorts. Then he chose a flannel shirt with long sleeves and lots of buttons. He wanted to show Muriel that when it came to buttons he meant business. He didn't bother to change his underclothes. In the top drawer his mother had laid out a new set for each day and marked that day on a small Post-it. Lenny ignored the Post-its.

Lenny tiptoed into the kitchen. His mother was standing in front of the open refrigerator with a carton of milk.

"Brr," said Lenny, sneaking up behind her.

Lenny's mother jumped. She dropped the milk carton.

"Whoops," said Lenny. "Sorry."

Lenny's mother grabbed a cloth and began wiping up spilled milk.

"Why are you wearing shorts in the middle of March?" she said to Lenny.

"I want to," said Lenny. "And Muriel said I could wear what I wanted. Did I tell you I met Muriel?"

"No, you didn't," said his mother, wringing the milk out of the cloth.

"Well, I'm telling you now," said Lenny. "I met Muriel. She's nice."

"I'm glad you like her," said Lenny's mother, slamming the refrigerator closed. The jars lined up on the inside of the door clanked like cymbals.

"Do that again," said Lenny.

Lenny's mother drove him to school and dropped him off.

"Have a nice day," she said, lifting a beige-gloved hand. It matched her sweater.

"You too," said Lenny. He stood in the playground, pushing his hands into his pockets. It was cold. His knees were freezing. The other children looked at him like he was an oddball. Some of them laughed. All because he was wearing shorts.

• • •

At lunchtime Lenny passed by Muriel to show her his outfit.

"I hate this game," he said.

"Why is that?" said Muriel.

"I want to call my mother and have her bring me my pants," said Lenny. "Why can't my mother choose my clothes?"

"Why do you want your mother to choose your clothes for you, Lenny?" asked Muriel. "You can do that."

"When my mother chooses my clothes, no one laughs," said Lenny.

"If you didn't want others laughing at you, why did you wear shorts?" asked Muriel.

"I don't know," said Lenny.

"Maybe you wanted them to laugh?" said Muriel.

"Maybe," said Lenny.

"And if you came to school dressed normally, they wouldn't laugh. They wouldn't pay attention to you," said Muriel.

"That's right," said Lenny.

"Are you sure laughing is the kind of attention you want?" asked Muriel.

"I don't want to be laughed at," said Lenny.

"No one wants to be laughed at," said Muriel. "Tomorrow, Lenny, think before choosing. Look at the weather. Think about what you're doing in school. Then make a better choice. I know you can do it, Lenny."

The next day, Lenny thought a little harder before dressing. He tried to recall what his mother had said about what matched and what didn't. But he couldn't remember. So he took out his book of flags. He thought no one would create a flag that people didn't like. A flag had to please all the citizens. So he decided that he'd put together his outfit like the colors of a flag.

Lenny closed his eyes and pointed randomly. His finger landed on the Italian flag. Green, white, and red. Lenny chose a pair of white pants and a green shirt with red stripes.

"I'm a flag," he said to himself, and he began swaying back and forth like a banner in the breeze. Lenny went to the kitchen, still swaying.

"Stop that, Lenny," said his mother. "You're making me dizzy."

"I'm a flag," said Lenny.

"Good for you," said his mother. She was sticking Post-it notes on the refrigerator, little reminders of what she had to do. She left them all over the house, little yellow flapping flags. Lenny thought his mother must like flags. That made him feel good.

"What are all these?" asked Lenny. He picked up a bottle of green liquid from a box sitting on the kitchen floor. There were sixteen bottles in all.

"Dishwashing liquid," said his mother. "I'm doing an ad for their product. This is how they thank me."

"Great," said Lenny. He screwed the top off a bottle and squeezed. Bubbles shot out of the opening and floated into the air. "Can I have one of these?" asked Lenny.

"Help yourself," said his mother.

Lenny took the bottle and squeezed out a few more bubbles. Then he puffed his cheeks out and exploded them with his hands.

"I thought you were a flag," said his mother.

"I changed my mind," said Lenny. "Now I'm a bubble."

5

Lenny waited in line for the bell to ring. No one seemed to be laughing at his clothes. No one seemed to be paying any attention to him at all. That made Lenny feel uncomfortable. Suddenly the cuffs of his shirt started to feel tight around his wrists. His pants felt rough against his skin. His socks were strangling his calves. Lenny bent over and rolled them down to his ankles.

During the math lesson, Lenny's ankles began to feel cold. So he leaned over and pulled his socks back up. He noticed they had red and green stripes across the tops. He hadn't seen that before.

"Hey," he said. "My socks match my outfit."

"Shh," said Ms. Schillinger.

Lenny sat quietly through English class. But during science he raised his hand.

"Why does popcorn pop?" he asked Ms. Schillinger.

Ms. Schillinger didn't know the answer. That always left Lenny feeling agitated. He hated not knowing the answer to things. At recess he asked if he could go to the library to find out.

"Go ahead, Leonard," said Ms. Schillinger.

Lenny found a book about corn. He turned to the index and found popcorn, page 38. Lenny opened to page 38 and read out loud: "Dried corn kernels contain a small quantity of water. When they are heated, the water turns to gas and the kernels explode."

"Like a fart," thought Lenny. Suddenly he started laughing.

"Shh," said Mrs. Marsh. She was the librarian.

But Lenny couldn't stop. He kept right on laughing.

"Lenny," said Mrs. Marsh. "This is a library, not a fun house."

Lenny just laughed harder. He laughed when Mrs. Marsh suggested that he leave the library. He laughed when she ushered him out the library door. And he laughed when she deposited him in Mr. Ourcival's office.

Lenny waited for the arrival of the king. That's how he thought of Mr. Ourcival. While he was waiting, he tried out the throne. He leaned to the left. Then he put his arms out to the sides and pretended he was flying. "Wheee," he said. He leaned back. "Watch out below."

Then Lenny hopped off the throne and walked over to the small square wooden chair with broken slats. Someone had carved the words "butt here" across the seat. Lenny set his bottom on the words.

Mr. Ourcival arrived. Lenny thought his tie looked too tight. It made Lenny feel as if someone were choking him.

"To what do I owe the honor of this visit?" asked Mr. Ourcival.

"I couldn't stop laughing," said Lenny.

"Maybe you'd like to share with us what you thought was so funny," said Mr. Ourcival.

Lenny wondered for a moment who the "us" was. He looked around to see if there was anyone else in the room.

"Not really," said Lenny.

"Mr. Brewster," said Mr. Ourcival. Lenny laughed again at Mr. Ourcival's calling him Mister.

"You can call me Lenny," he said.

Mr. Ourcival didn't answer with words. But Lenny saw his body stiffen. He thought what Mr. Ourcival needed was to throw himself onto the floor in a game of Twister.

Mr. Ourcival sat down in his big overblown chair. It sank under his weight.

"What a waste," thought Lenny. "A chair that does all those things and he doesn't even take advantage of it." Lenny stopped a minute to think of all the brainpower that went into inventing the different kinds of chairs in the world. Chairs that could spin. Chairs that moved up and down like those at the barbershop or dentist's office. Reclining chairs. Chairs for babies. He began thinking about the kind of chair that he might invent. Then he remembered a line from a book he'd read about inventions improving civilization. "Could a chair improve civilization?" he thought.

"I wonder if you'll find cleaning the playground after school as amusing as the library," said Mr. Ourcival.

"Beats me," said Lenny.

He left Mr. Ourcival's office wondering if the world would be a better place if everyone had a throne or a chair that could spin around.

• • •

"Do you think a chair could improve civilization?" asked Lenny.

"I'm not sure exactly what you mean," said Muriel.

"I think if everyone had a chair that could spin and they spun around a few times a day, they might be nicer," said Lenny. "I think it would make them happier."

"That could be," said Muriel.

"You know what centrifugal force is?" asked Lenny.

"Tell me," said Muriel.

"It's when you get going really fast and move away from the center," said Lenny. "If I keep going faster, I'm going to end up in your lap."

"That reminds me a little of life," said Muriel.

"How's that?" said Lenny.

"Well," said Muriel, "in life you start with a very small circle where just you fit in. Then, as you get bigger, the circle grows and widens until it includes other people." Muriel spun around slowly in her chair. On the back was a bumper sticker. EMPATHY.

"What's empathy?" asked Lenny.

"Empathy is the ability to participate in others' feelings," said Muriel. "Not just knowing how they feel, but actually feeling it."

"Would that be like when I looked at Mr. Ourcival's tie and I felt like I was choking?" said Lenny.

"Sort of," said Muriel. "But that's a little different. Do you find Mr. Ourcival frightening?"

"He never laughs," said Lenny.

"He thinks you laugh too much," said Muriel. "What was so funny yesterday, Lenny? So funny that you disturbed Mrs. Marsh and the other students in the library?"

"I don't know," said Lenny.

"Yes you do, Lenny," said Muriel. "You must know. Mrs. Marsh said you laughed the entire time you were there. You laughed all the way to Mr. Ourcival's office."

"I just like laughing," said Lenny.

"Does laughing make you feel good, Lenny?" asked Muriel.

"Yup," said Lenny.

"It makes me feel good, too," said Muriel. "But you can't go through life laughing."

"Why not?" said Lenny.

"You know, Lenny," said Muriel. "Laughter is a way of expressing how you feel. Like crying."

"I never cry," said Lenny.

"Never?" asked Muriel.

"Nope," said Lenny.

"I think everyone cries sometimes," said Muriel.

"Not me," said Lenny.

"Well, I'll bet you're the only one in the world," said Muriel.

"Could be," said Lenny.

• • •

For a couple of seconds Lenny liked being the only one in the world. That made him stand out. But then he was seized with a feeling of loneliness. Like a solitary ship on an endless sea. It wasn't the idea of not having anyone to talk to that bothered him. What really bothered Lenny was the idea that there'd be no one there to listen.

6

Petrified chewing gum, peanut butter smears, a stray marble, a pink barrette, mangled swings, birds picking at snack crumbs sprinkled across the pavement. All remnants of a good time. It was a very satisfying feeling to take in the empty playground at the end of the day. Lenny grabbed the bucket of water and the sponge and cloth that the janitor had given him and headed straight for the slippery slide. Lenny was an expert on slides. Of all the pieces of playground equipment, they got the worst beating. And a clean slide was essential for a good ride. One person with muddy treads slowed down the whole descent.

Lenny stopped for a look. Sure enough, the slide was streaked with mud. Lenny started to rub it off with a wet sponge. He began to hum to himself. He didn't mind the work. Halfway down the slide, he took a break and skipped over to the monkey bars. He swung from them, lifting his feet off the ground into the air. He felt free. Like a bird. He let go, jumping as far as he could. Then he went back to the slide. After several minutes, he noticed that he was being watched. There was a small boy squinting up at him. He was smiling.

"What are you staring at?" Lenny asked.

"Nothing," said the boy. He was about the size of a seven-year-old. But his face looked older. Lenny went back to work, but the boy didn't budge. He stood patiently watching.

"Waiting for something?" asked Lenny.

"I'm just waiting to use the slide," said the boy. Lenny finished rinsing the ladder rungs.

"I'm almost done," he said. Then he stood back to admire his work.

"Can I go now?" asked the boy.

"We'd better dry it first," said Lenny. He wiped the slide with a cloth. "Okay," he said.

He watched the boy climb up the ladder. The boy stopped for a second at the top. Then he slipped down slowly, hands gripping the sides, like someone sliding into oblivion.

"Didn't anyone ever teach you how to go down a slide?" Lenny asked.

The boy looked puzzled. Lenny bounded up the ladder. He grabbed the sides and threw himself into the descent. He raised his hands into the air and shouted "Whoa!" as he flew down. "Now you try," he said to the boy.

The boy climbed the ladder a little more quickly than before. This time he slid down and let his hands go. But his sneakers caught against the metal sides.

"Lift your feet," said Lenny. "And your hands. Be like a plane taking off."

The boy did as Lenny instructed, and this time he went faster, flying off the end of the slide and bouncing back onto his feet.

"Do you go to this school?" Lenny asked. He didn't think he'd seen the boy before.

"No," said the boy. "I go to Vine Street School."

"Oh," said Lenny. Vine Street School was three blocks away. He felt a slight pang of disappointment. It wasn't every day that he found someone with a true appreciation of a slippery slide.

"What's your name?" asked Lenny.

"Vander James," said the boy. "But you can call me Van."

"Are you sure your name isn't the other way around?" said Lenny. "James Vander sounds better."

"I'm sure," said the boy.

"Well, I'm Lenny Brewster," said Lenny. "You can call me Lenny." Lenny stopped to think what it would be like if he were called Brewster Lenny. The thought made him laugh.

Van grinned widely. But despite his smile, he had a permanent look of worry on his face.

Van looked at his watch. "I have to go," he said.

"See you later," said Lenny, emptying the bucket of water onto the pavement. It made several small puddles. Lenny tossed a pebble into the biggest. He marveled at the way the water formed rings and rippled outward. Then Lenny jumped into the puddle himself. The water sprayed into the air.

"It's raining!" cried Lenny.

7

"Did you choose those clothes, Lenny?" asked Muriel.

"Yup," said Lenny. "Wasn't that part of the game?"

"Yes," said Muriel.

"Do I remind you of anything?" asked Lenny. "Like the Estonian flag?"

"How's the Estonian flag?" asked Muriel.

"It's blue, black, and white," said Lenny. "Just like how I'm dressed."

"I didn't know that, Lenny," said Muriel.

"Well, now you do," said Lenny. "Hey, do you have any flags on your shelf?" he asked.

"I don't think so," said Muriel.

Lenny stood up and walked over to Muriel's shelves. He picked up a small clown that was wearing white gloves. It had a key in its back. Lenny wound up the key.

"You know how this works?" he asked.

"Why don't you tell me," said Muriel.

"There's a spring inside," said Lenny. "And when I

turn the key, it winds up tighter and tighter. Then, when I stop, it unwinds and the clown starts to move."

Lenny watched the clown spin around in circles, waving its hands in the air.

"Can I put this clown in my space?" asked Lenny. "It reminds me of my mother."

"What's your mom like, Lenny?" asked Muriel.

"She's like that windup clown," said Lenny.

"In what way?" asked Muriel. "You mean she's funny?"

"She can be pretty funny," said Lenny. "But I was thinking how she moves fast. I guess it's because she's always busy. She has a lot to do."

"I'll bet she does," said Muriel. "She needs to look after you. And maybe the rest of your family."

"There is no rest of my family," said Lenny.

"No brothers or sisters?" asked Muriel.

"Nope," said Lenny.

"No dad?" said Muriel.

"I don't have a dad," said Lenny.

"No?" said Muriel.

"I do have one, but he doesn't live with us," said Lenny.

"Where does he live?" asked Muriel.

"He went up in a space shuttle and is still orbiting around somewhere," said Lenny.

"He's an astronaut, then?" said Muriel.

"Not really," said Lenny.

"What's he doing in space?" asked Muriel.

"He just got up there and he can't get back. You know, because of no gravity. He's just stuck up there forever."

"Do you think he's ever coming back?" asked Muriel.

"I don't think he can ever get through that barrier," said Lenny.

"That must make you sad," said Muriel.

"Yup," said Lenny.

"Maybe someday you'll be able to break through that barrier and get to him," said Muriel.

"You think so?" asked Lenny.

"Maybe," said Muriel.

Lenny went back over to the shelf of objects and picked up a small rock.

"Think this could be a space rock?" he asked.

"I don't think it came from space," said Muriel. "But if you'd like, we can say it's a space rock. This is your space and you're making the rules."

"Okay," said Lenny. He took the rock and put it on the next shelf, above the jumping bean and the clown.

"I have to put this a little higher," he said. "Because it's a space rock and it has to be in space. Space is in another atmosphere."

"All right," said Muriel. "You can do that."

8

Lenny unscrewed the top off a cookie. He looked at the round flat circle of vanilla cream in the middle. "How do you think they get this so perfect? So round? So flat?" he asked.

"No clue," said his mother. She took a bundle of clothes out of the dryer and began folding them.

"I bet they have a machine that does it," said Lenny. "I'd like to see that machine."

"Me too," said his mother halfheartedly, pulling the lint from the filter.

"Did I tell you I got to visit Mr. Ourcival the other day?" said Lenny.

"No, you didn't," said his mother. "But the principal's office did. They called to tell me you'd be home late from school."

"Did they tell you why?" asked Lenny.

"They said you'd been disruptive in the library," said his mother.

"Did they tell you I was laughing?" said Lenny. "And I couldn't stop?"

"What do you mean, you couldn't stop?" asked his mother.

"I just couldn't," said Lenny.

"That's not funny," said his mother.

"Mr. Ourcival didn't think it was funny either," said Lenny. He screwed the top off another cookie. "Anyway, I got sent out to clean the playground and I met somebody. Want to know who?"

"Who?" said his mother.

"Van," said Lenny. "I think he's a little younger than me, but he looks older."

"Does he act a lot older?" asked Lenny's mother.

"Don't know yet," said Lenny. "Probably."

"Great," said his mother. "I hope you become good friends."

"Me too," said Lenny, stuffing the cookie halves into his mouth.

Lenny stepped out of his clothes. Red and blue and white. Today he'd been the flag of Panama. He walked over and around them a few times. Then he rolled them into a ball and carried them into the bathroom. One by one he tossed them into the dirty clothes basket. He overshot the socks and thought of leaving them where they'd landed. But then he changed his mind and picked them up.

Lenny climbed in between the covers of his bed. His mother had tucked the sheets a little too tightly, so he felt wrapped up like a mummy.

Above Lenny's bed was a poster of the starship *Enterprise*. Lenny loved that poster. He liked to imagine that he was captain of the *Enterprise*. Who knew what was out there in space? Besides his father. He'd left when Lenny was two years old, and no one had heard from him since. Lenny had convinced himself that he was lost in space. Because if he were here on this earth, why wasn't he with Lenny? As brilliant as Lenny was, he could not find the answer to this question.

• • •

"How's it going at home?" asked Muriel.

"Great," said Lenny. "I got my own breakfast this morning."

"Good for you," said Muriel.

"You haven't happened to see my friend Van anywhere around?" asked Lenny.

"I didn't know you had a friend named Van," said Muriel.

"I met him at the playground the other day," said

Lenny. "By the slide. You know how to slide, don't you, Muriel?"

"I used to," said Muriel.

"Because if you don't, I can teach you," said Lenny.

"Thank you," said Muriel. "I'll remember that."

"Van didn't know a thing about sliding," said Lenny. "But I showed him how to do it right."

"That was nice of you, Lenny," said Muriel.

"He's a small guy," said Lenny. "But his face looks kind of old. He was smiling, though. He looked happy."

"I don't think I've seen anyone who fits that description," said Muriel.

"I was just wondering," said Lenny. "If you do, you could tell him I said hello."

"I'll do that," said Muriel.

"And you can tell him he's a pretty good slider, too," said Lenny.

"Okay," said Muriel.

• • •

At recess, Lenny hung on the monkey bars. Then he walked over to the slide. It was free. Lenny slid down a couple of times. He wondered if they even had a slide at the Vine Street School.

Lenny walked by a group of boys who were swapping

dragon cards. Lenny moved a little closer. No one paid any attention to him. That's because he didn't have any of those cards with dragons—the ones with dozens of claws, double-edged teeth, and fire coming out of their noses. He thought they were stupid.

Back in class, Lenny took his math paper and folded it into a jet. He parked it on the corner of his desk, on an imaginary runway. He'd folded it so the numbers 747 showed on the side. Lenny admired the plane. Suddenly he couldn't resist. He picked up the plane and launched it. It sailed and dipped, coming to a halt in the center of Ms. Schillinger's desk, right next to her coffee mug, which had pink lipstick around the rim. Lenny wondered if it was strawberry-flavored lipstick. His mother had some of that, and it smelled terrific.

"Smooth flight," said Lenny. "No wind today." Lenny had been on a plane a couple of times. He tried to remember what the pilot had said. "Clear day, folks. Cruising altitude of—"

Ms. Schillinger interrupted him. "Ground control to Leonard Brewster," she said. "We're talking about fractions and not the weather," she said.

"Sorry," said Lenny. He looked out the window. He wondered which direction the wind was blowing. Some trees were swaying to the left, others to the right. There were cross-breezes. Lenny wondered how they measured wind speed when there were cross-breezes.

• • •

"Ms. Schillinger doesn't like my demonstrations," said Lenny.

"I'm sure she does," said Muriel. "But not while she's trying to teach. There's a time and place for them, Lenny. And if you can learn to pay attention to that, Ms. Schillinger will appreciate your demonstrations much more."

"It's just that I can't help it," said Lenny.

"What can't you help?" said Muriel.

"I think about something and I just have to do it," said Lenny. "Or else I feel like I'll explode."

"Let's try an experiment," said Muriel.

"I love experiments," said Lenny.

"I know you do," said Muriel. "So try this. The next time you feel like you're going to explode, take a deep breath. Then slowly let the air out."

"Like a balloon," said Lenny.

"Yes," said Muriel. "Slowly, slowly, let go of it. Pretend you're a balloon if that helps. Can you do that and let me know what happens?"

"Sure I can," said Lenny. "You haven't happened to see anyone who looked like he could be Van, have you?"

"No," said Muriel. "But I'll let you know if I do."

9

Lenny sat in class. Ms. Schillinger was explaining how the pyramids were built: how the Egyptians used levers to lift the two-ton stones that were their building blocks.

"I know, I know, I know," Lenny kept saying to himself. He was dying to make a lever. He was sure he could lift his desk with one finger and his metal ruler. He reached into the pocket of his desk and got the ruler. As he looked around for something he could use as a fulcrum, he remembered what Muriel had said.

Lenny put down the ruler. He took a deep breath and let it out slowly. It was kind of fun. Lenny took another breath. This time he made a little sound as he let it out. The sound got deeper as the breath grew more shallow.

"Stop breathing so loudly," said Margery. She sat across from Lenny.

"Are you all right, Leonard?" asked Ms. Schillinger. She actually seemed worried.

"I'm fine," said Lenny.

"He's choking on his eraser," said Will.

"No I'm not," said Lenny. He held his pencil in the air. The eraser was still intact.

Lenny put the ruler back in his desk and focused on the poster of the pyramid hanging at the front of the room. It was a big triangle made of blocks with a small rectangular entrance. Lenny imagined stepping into the pyramid. Suddenly his breathing became normal, but his thoughts were still racing. He wondered if it was hot inside the pyramid.

• • •

"It worked," said Lenny.

"What worked?" asked Muriel.

"The experiment," said Lenny. "The breathing thing. I just let my breath out slowly, and then I didn't feel like I'd explode anymore."

"You see, Lenny," said Muriel. "You've discovered something new. You can control some of your feelings so they don't get out of hand."

"Ms. Schillinger was worried something might be wrong with me," said Lenny.

"There's nothing wrong with you, Lenny," said Muriel.

"Not with my breathing, anyway," said Lenny.

"Not with anything," said Muriel.

"I was wondering if it was hot in those pyramids," said Lenny. "I think it must have been. What do you think, Muriel?"

"I think you're probably right," said Muriel.

• • •

Lenny stood at the corner waiting to cross the street. He noticed that the crossing lady was dressed in red, white, yellow, and blue. Like the Malaysian flag.

Lenny started across the street, moving quickly. Then suddenly his attention was caught by something and he slowed. He crouched down.

"Lenny," said the crossing lady.

Lenny didn't get up. He tipped his head to the side until it nearly touched the ground.

"Is he okay?" asked one of the older children crossing the street.

"I'm sure he's fine," said the crossing lady.

Lenny was looking under a car that was pulled to a halt at the crosswalk. "Hey, that guy's about to lose his muffler," he said.

A horn blew.

"Hurry up, Lenny," said the crossing lady. "You're holding up traffic."

"Did you see that guy's muffler?" said Lenny.

"No, I didn't," said the crossing lady, who seemed to

have other things on her mind. "If I were looking under cars, you'd all be under cars."

"You're funny," said Lenny.

Lenny walked on by himself. He couldn't figure out why no one was interested in the muffler but him. Lenny turned and watched the car pick up speed. He leaned over for another look. Then he shrugged and turned the corner. There was Van, sitting on a bench.

"Hey, Van," said Lenny. "Remember me, Lenny?"

"Sure," said Van. He was still smiling.

"What are you doing here?" asked Lenny.

"I'm waiting for my dad," said Van.

"Did you see that guy dragging his muffler?" said Lenny, turning to look back. "Hey, here he comes." Lenny pointed to the light blue car creeping along in their direction.

"That's my dad," said Van.

"Better tell him he needs a new muffler," said Lenny. "I can spot a low muffler anywhere."

"Thanks, Lenny," said Van. He got up and started toward the car.

"Where are you going?" asked Lenny.

"I have to go get a shot," said Van.

"Ouch!" shouted Lenny.

Van laughed. "Maybe I'll see you again," he said.

Van climbed into the car and drove off. He stuck his hand out the window and waved. Lenny waved back.

"Van's father needs a new muffler," said Lenny.

"So you found your friend, Van," said Muriel.

"Yup," said Lenny. "He better get that new muffler soon, or else."

"Or else what?" asked Muriel.

"Or else he's going to be making sparks when that muffler touches the ground," said Lenny.

"Would you like to see that?" asked Muriel.

"Sure," said Lenny. "Who wouldn't? It's like fireworks. But I think he needs to get it checked out. While he's at it, he probably needs to get the whole car checked out."

"Why is that?" asked Muriel.

"Because maybe there's something else wrong with it," said Lenny. "Something more serious. I mean, what would happen if the brakes were worn and they were driving really fast and couldn't stop?"

"What would happen?" asked Muriel.

"They might crash and get hurt. They might even die," said Lenny.

"That worries you, doesn't it, Lenny?" said Muriel.

"A little," said Lenny. "I wouldn't want Van to die. Or his dad either."

"I'm sure you wouldn't," said Muriel. "They probably won't, though, Lenny. And I'm sure when they get the muffler fixed, the mechanic will check out the whole car."

"They're going to die someday, though," said Lenny. "Everybody does."

"That's right, Lenny," said Muriel. "Does that worry you?"

"You mean dying?" asked Lenny.

"Yes," said Muriel.

"My grandfather died," said Lenny.

"When was that?" asked Muriel.

"When I was six," said Lenny. "He was sick. Really sick. He was like a big round lollipop slowly sucked away until it wasn't anymore."

"I bet that was awful for you, Lenny," said Muriel.

"It was, but I'm not going to say any more because you might start crying," said Lenny.

"I might," said Muriel, "because it's sad. Would it bother you if I cried?"

"I hate when people cry," said Lenny.

"Does it make you want to cry?" asked Muriel.

"Nope," said Lenny. "Hey, you remember that empathy thing you were telling me about?"

"Yes," said Muriel.

"I had some for Van today," said Lenny. "He had to have a shot. I hate shots. I hate sharp pointed needles. When Van told me, I got goose bumps. It was like I was going to have the shot."

"That's empathy, Lenny," said Muriel.

"Well, I had some today," said Lenny.

"That's good," said Muriel. "Are you going to see Van again?"

"I don't know where he lives," said Lenny. "I forgot to ask. Hey, maybe I could look it up in the phone book."

"Why not?" said Muriel. "Do you know his last name?"

"James," said Lenny.

"James is a common name," said Muriel. "There might be quite a few of them in the phone book. But I think you should give it a try."

Lenny got up and walked over to Muriel's bookshelf. He picked up a little rubber man whose arms and legs could bend in any direction. He was wearing a big smile.

"Do you want to add him to your space?" asked Muriel.

"I'm not going to put him there yet," said Lenny. "But I'm going to put him nearby. And I'm going to take this marble, too."

Lenny picked up a cat's-eye with green and white flecks.

"I used to play marbles with my grandfather," said Lenny. "Where do you think I should put this marble, Muriel? My grandfather's dead and he's underground. But you don't have a shelf down there."

"Just because he's dead, Lenny, doesn't mean you can't put him in your space," said Muriel. "When people die, we don't forget all about them. Part of them stays very much alive in our hearts and our heads."

Lenny put the marble on the shelf close to where he was standing. "It looks like an eye," said Lenny. "It's looking at me."

10

Lenny took the phone book from the top of the refrigerator where his mother kept it. He turned to the "J's" and ran his finger down the page until he came to the name James. There were sixteen of them. The last was Vander James. Lenny wondered if Van had his own phone. Or maybe his father's name was Van, too. Or maybe there was another Vander James. Lenny thought this was unlikely, but he enjoyed reviewing the possibilities in his head.

The address for Vander James was 5 Pearl Street. Pearl Street was on the other side of the playground.

"Lenny," called his mother. "Are you ready?"

"Yup," said Lenny. He closed the phone book and left it on the kitchen table. Then he followed his mother out to the car.

Lenny climbed into the backseat. Mrs. Ashe was in the front. She was Lenny's elderly neighbor. Lenny's mother took her grocery shopping on Thursdays.

Lenny stared at the back of Mrs. Ashe's head, at her

bob of thinning gray hair. It was actually more blue than gray. Lenny wondered if it was real or colored. He didn't think real hair came in that shade.

Mrs. Ashe carried a cane, which Lenny now held across his lap. Lenny stroked the cane. It was smooth and worn. And it was light when he lifted it. He thought that was what old weak bones must feel like. Lenny looked at the skin on Mrs. Ashe's neck: thin and transparent. He thought he never wanted to grow old.

"Can you drop me at the playground?" said Lenny. Lenny's mother thought for a moment. She tightened her grip on the steering wheel. Lenny looked at her hands. She was wearing dark red leather gloves. Her driving gloves, she called them. But she wore them when she shopped, too. Shopping meant a lot of hand work— choosing, bagging, carrying items.

"All right," said Lenny's mother. "But be careful."

"You mean don't go down the slide headfirst on my back?" said Lenny.

"Exactly," said Lenny's mother. Mrs. Ashe laughed. Lenny watched her body shake. Like Jell-O, he thought.

Lenny hopped out of the car.

"I'll be back to get you in about an hour," said his mother.

"Okay," said Lenny. He set the alarm on his watch and skipped over to the swings.

There was a playground monitor, so it would have

been hard for Lenny to go down the slide headfirst. Anyway, Lenny didn't plan on staying at the playground long. He went over to the slide and whizzed down a couple of times. Then he wandered out of the playground and over to Pearl Street. Five was the second house from the corner. Lenny walked up the steps and rang the bell.

The door opened. It was Van.

"Surprise!" said Lenny.

"Oh, hi," said Van. "How did you know where I lived?"

"I looked it up in the phone book," said Lenny. "Vander James, five Pearl Street."

"That's my dad," said Van.

"That's what I thought," said Lenny. "Are you happy to see me?"

Van nodded. "Do you want to come in?" he said.

"I can just stay a little while," said Lenny. "My mother's at the grocery store."

"Who is it?" asked a lady coming into the hallway. She was dressed in a nurse's uniform.

"That's my mom," said Van.

"I guess she's a nurse. Or else she's playing dress-up," said Lenny.

Van laughed. "She's a nurse," he said.

"This is Lenny," said Van to his mother. "He's my friend. I met him at the playground."

"At the slide," said Lenny, wanting to be precise.

"Hello, Lenny," said Mrs. James. "Nice to meet you. Does your mother know you're here?"

"She's at the grocery store," said Van.

"She's picking me up later," said Lenny.

Van's father appeared next. He was wearing a blue tie with dolphins leaping across it. He was a big man, very tall. And he was smiling just like Van.

"So who's this young man?" asked Mr. James.

"This is Lenny," said Van's mother.

"Glad to know you, Lenny," said Van's father. He reached his hand out, and Lenny shook it. It was a firm hand. And gloveless. "So you're the mechanic."

"I told him about the muffler," said Van.

"Good thing," said Lenny.

"You'll be glad to know I'm taking the car in tomorrow," said Mr. James.

"They'll put it up on one of those hydraulic lifts," said Lenny to Van. "And hopefully they'll check out everything while you're there."

"I'm sure they will," said Mr. James.

"Good," said Lenny, feeling relieved.

Van led Lenny down the hallway and up a flight of stairs. At the top was a baby's crib. Van stopped to peek in. A baby girl was sucking happily on a pacifier. Lenny liked the sound she made.

"That's Audrey," said Van, poking the baby in the belly. "She's my little sister."

"Hi, Audrey," said Lenny.

Audrey spit out her pacifier and grabbed hold of her toes. Then she pulled one to her mouth.

"Yummy," said Lenny. He thought Audrey was cute.

"She likes you," said Van.

"How do you know?" asked Lenny.

"She only spits out her pacifier at people she likes," said Van.

"Oh," said Lenny. He wondered why that was.

Van led Lenny down a corridor. They passed a table covered with bottles and packets of gauze and cotton. There were even a couple of syringes. The odor of rubbing alcohol permeated the air. Lenny slowed down. He picked up a small box from the table.

"What's this?" he asked.

"That's a pill crusher," said Van.

"How does it work?" asked Lenny.

"Like this," said Van. He took a pill from a bottle and dropped it into the box. Then he squeezed down the top. When he opened the box, the pill had been crushed into a fine powder.

"That's neat," said Lenny. He looked back at the table. "Are all these things real?" he asked.

"Yes," said Van.

"Gee, then someone around here must be really sick,"

said Lenny. He looked back down the corridor at Audrey's crib.

"Someone is," said Van.

"Who?" asked Lenny. Van's parents didn't look sick. Nor did Audrey. Lenny's eyes rested for a moment on Van: his thin hair, his pale skin, his small size.

"Me," said Van.

"Oh," said Lenny. "What's wrong with you?"

"I have a blood disease," said Van.

Lenny had never known anyone who was really sick before, except for his grandfather. But that was different. He was old.

"I have leukemia," said Van. Then he smiled. "But I'm almost cured," he added cheerfully.

"Phew," said Lenny. That made him feel better. He picked up a syringe with a needle attached. Goose bumps broke out on his skin. "I hate needles," he said.

"Me too," said Van.

Lenny put down the syringe. He followed Van into his room.

They were welcomed by a small robot. Van leaned down and flipped a switch on its back. It began running circles around Lenny.

Lenny picked up the robot. The legs kept on kicking in midair. Its arms waved frantically for a few seconds, then ran down to a gentle wag.

"The battery's low," said Van.

Lenny turned the robot over and flipped off the switch. Then he laid it on Van's bed. He looked around. Van had a window carved in the middle of his ceiling. It was a skylight.

"I like your window," said Lenny pointing upward.

"At night I can see the stars and sometimes the moon," said Van.

"Does it open?" asked Lenny.

"Just a crack," said Van.

Lenny walked to a corner of Van's room where there was a tower made of wooden blocks.

"What are you making?" he asked.

"A tower," said Van. "It starts in the basement, and I'm going to build it all the way up to the ceiling."

"I'd like to see that," said Lenny.

"Okay," said Van.

Van took Lenny down to the basement. It smelled of laundry detergent and apples. Lenny loved apples.

"Over there," said Van.

Beside the washing machine was the base of the tower. It was thick at the bottom and thinned out as it rose upward.

"It goes right through my father's study upstairs," said Van. "Then up to my room."

"Amazing," said Lenny. "Where'd you get all these blocks?"

"My dad made them," said Van.

"Oh," said Lenny. "That was really nice of him."

"He likes woodworking," said Van.

For a moment Lenny felt sorry for himself. He not only didn't have any blocks, but didn't have a father to make them.

Van led Lenny up the stairs and into his father's study, where the tower continued. It looked to be growing out of the floorboards and reached all the way up to the ceiling.

"Wouldn't it be neat if you could build it right out the window and into space," said Lenny.

"It would," said Van. "But I don't think I can."

"You can try," said Lenny.

"Anyway, my dad has to make more blocks," said Van, leading Lenny back to his room. He opened a cupboard under his desk. On a shelf was a row of Lego planes.

"Did you build those?" asked Lenny.

"Yes," said Van. "I love to build things."

"Me too," said Lenny.

Surrounding the planes was a group of small rubber dinosaurs, all different colors. Lenny picked up a blue one with spikes running down its spine.

"They bounce," said Van.

Lenny dropped the dinosaur and watched it bounce to a stop. Van bounced a red one. Then the alarm on Lenny's watch went off.

"Time to go," said Lenny. He followed Van back

down the corridor, past the table with the pill crusher. He tried not to look. But suddenly it seemed like everything on that table was alive—the needles, the pills, the gauze. Lenny walked faster.

"Bye," he said to Audrey as he passed the crib.

"Bye," he said to Mr. and Mrs. James, who weren't even in sight.

11

Lenny walked back to the playground. He climbed the ladder of the slide. Then he slid down as slowly as possible, pushing his elbows against the metal sides. He did that on purpose. When he got to the bottom, he sat for a few seconds in the metal lap of the slide.

Lenny's mother pulled up to the curb. "Lenny!" she hollered.

Lenny went over to the car and climbed in. Mrs. Ashe was crunching on some potato chips. Lenny wondered if her teeth were real. He'd seen a lot of advertisements on television for cream to hold in false teeth. He figured old people must lose a lot of their teeth.

"Would you like one?" Mrs. Ashe asked Lenny.

"No, thanks," said Lenny.

Lenny was quiet at dinner. No balancing of forks on glasses. No rocking backward on the chair. No questions about how this or that worked.

"Are you all right, Lenny?" asked his mother.

"Sure I'm all right," said Lenny. "Don't I look okay?"

Lenny couldn't rid himself of the image of the table at Van's house with the pills and the shots and the smell of rubbing alcohol.

"You're awfully quiet," said his mother. She sounded worried.

Lenny began to tap his fork against his glass. He hoped that might ease his mother's concern.

After dinner Lenny went to his room. He took out his box of Lego bricks and began to build an aircraft, one with wings that you could reposition. Lenny glided his aircraft around the room on imaginary currents of air. Then suddenly Lenny felt something building up inside of him. It wasn't long before he felt like he might explode. He took a deep breath as Muriel had said, and let it out slowly. Then he took another. But this time it didn't work. Lenny smashed the aircraft into the wall. He watched the pieces tumble and crash to the floor.

"What's going on up there?" hollered Lenny's mother from the bottom of the stairs.

"Nothing much," said Lenny. "A plane just crashed." Lenny felt that something else had collapsed, too. Something inside of him. But he wasn't sure what.

• • •

"I don't like old people," said Lenny.

"Why don't you like old people?" asked Muriel.

"They're kind of scary," said Lenny. "They're all wrinkled, and their bones look like they're going to break. Their teeth are falling out."

"A lot of old people have their teeth," said Muriel.

"I'm not ever going to get old," said Lenny.

"But you are," said Muriel.

"Nope," said Lenny. "Not if I can help it."

"That's the thing, Lenny," said Muriel. "You can't help it. It doesn't matter what age you are in your head. Someday your body is going to slow down. It's going to age. That's what life is."

"I don't like life," said Lenny.

Lenny got up and walked over to his space. He wound up the key on the clown with the white gloves. Then he clapped his hands and watched the jumping bean pop into the air.

"I think I'm going to add something," said Lenny.

"Anything you like," said Muriel.

Lenny took five small colored wooden blocks from a shelf and stacked them one on top of the other. Then he took the rubber man and set him on top of the highest block. His smiling face was turned upward toward the space rock.

"I'm done," said Lenny.

"Do you want to explain what the blocks are?" asked Muriel.

"No," said Lenny.

"Do you know what leukemia is?" Lenny asked.

"Leukemia is a disease of the blood," said Muriel. "It's a form of cancer."

"Do you know anyone who has it?" asked Lenny.

"I don't," said Muriel.

"I do," said Lenny. "He lives here, in this town. But he goes to a different school."

"I'm sorry to hear that, Lenny," said Muriel.

"It's sad," said Lenny.

"I think so," said Muriel.

"You have to take a lot of pills and have a lot of shots," said Lenny. "And you look kind of sick all of the time. Do you think it hurts?" he asked.

"Sometimes," said Muriel. "Maybe it's not pain like a headache or a broken bone. But I'm sure it must hurt inside."

"Do you think it could hurt somebody else inside?" asked Lenny.

"You mean like you, Lenny?" asked Muriel.

"Yes," said Lenny.

"I think it can," said Muriel. "That's empathy. That's what we talked about before. Can you tell me who this is? It sounds like you know the person pretty well."

"It's Vander James," said Lenny.

"You mean your new friend, Van?" asked Muriel.

"Yup," said Lenny. "And it makes me mad."

"I'm sure it does," said Muriel. "And sad and confused and scared and a lot of other things, too. Those feelings are normal, Lenny."

Lenny spun around in the chair a couple of times.

"I wish Van could see this chair," he said. "I bet if he spun around a few times he'd feel a lot better."

"Why don't you spin around a few times for Van?" said Muriel.

"Okay," said Lenny, pushing off for a couple of rounds.

"Do you feel better?" asked Muriel.

"A little," said Lenny.

12

Lenny took out his whoopee cushion and placed it under the flat pillow on one of the kitchen chairs. It was the chair that Lenny was going to offer to Van. Van was coming over to his house to play. Lenny looked at the clock. It was ten to four. Van was due at four. Lenny had set the alarm clock. Then he'd watched his mother make the fastest batch of brownies in the world.

"Want to help, Lenny?" she'd asked. But before Lenny could pitch in, she'd already finished mixing the batter. Lenny got to lick the beaters.

At four Lenny's alarm clock went off, then the buzzer on the stove.

Lenny's mother hurried back into the kitchen. "That isn't the smoke alarm, is it?" she said.

"No," said Lenny. "It's the alarm on my watch. Van's late. I hope he's all right."

"I'm sure he's okay," said Lenny's mother. But Lenny wasn't so sure.

Van showed up at four-ten. He had his robot with

him—and his mother. She wanted to meet Lenny's mother.

"You're a little late," said Lenny, pulling Van into the kitchen. He left his mother to talk with Mrs. James.

"Sorry," said Van.

"Want a brownie?" asked Lenny. "We made them just for you."

"Thanks," said Van, sitting down in the chair Lenny motioned to.

The whoopee cushion let out a long low fart.

"What was that?" asked Van, hopping to his feet.

"You farted," said Lenny. "P.U.!"

Van started to laugh. He lifted the pillow off the chair and pulled out the whoopee cushion. Then he began bouncing on it.

Lenny's mother came into the kitchen.

"So how are you, Van?" she asked.

"Fine," said Van.

"I made you boys brownies," said Lenny's mother. "Help yourselves."

"I am," said Van. "They're delicious."

Lenny's mother was wearing a pair of beige gloves. Van looked at them curiously.

"I bet you're wondering why my mother is wearing gloves," said Lenny, when his mother had left the room.

"Maybe her hands are cold," said Van.

"It's because she's a hand model," said Lenny. "She has

to keep her hands in perfect shape. Otherwise she won't get any work."

"What's a hand model?" asked Van.

"She does advertisements for jewelry and bread and soap, and stuff like that," said Lenny. "Anything you have to hold. I bet you've seen her a million times on TV."

Van's face lit up. "She's on TV?" he said.

"Her hands are," said Lenny.

"I never knew of anyone who did that," said Van. "Or anyone on TV."

"Well, now you do," said Lenny.

Van got up and walked over to the window. It was decked with plants. Lenny's mother loved plants. There were tubes that wound like snakes from one pot to the next.

"What are all those tubes?" asked Van.

Lenny had constructed an automatic water system with rubber tubing and metal washers. All Lenny's mother had to do was pour the water into a central vase and it branched out to all the plants.

"It's an automatic watering system," said Lenny. "I made it."

"You did?" said Van.

Lenny poured a pitcher of water into the large vase beside the window.

Van got down on his hands and knees and followed

the trail of water that bubbled from the base of one pot to another.

"You're really smart," said Van.

"Thank you," said Lenny.

Lenny took Van to his room. His book of flags lay open on his desk.

"Are you studying flags?" asked Van.

"I'm working on it," said Lenny, looking down at his clothes. Today he was dressed like the flag of Argentina. Blue and white.

In the corner was Lenny's current project: a collection of empty cardboard toilet paper rolls that he had just begun painting.

"What are you doing with all those?" asked Van.

"I don't know yet," said Lenny.

"They'd make an amazing tower," said Van. "I could help if you want."

"But we've got to finish painting them first," said Lenny.

"I love to paint," said Van.

"Okay," said Lenny. He took out his box of paints, twelve wafer-shaped rounds of color, and brushes. "I have to put newspaper down or else my mother gets mad," he said. Then he got two cups of water.

"I like that color green," said Van.

"It's dragon green," said Lenny.

Van dipped his brush in the round of paint. "I don't think there're any such things as dragons," said Van.

"Well, it's the color they'd be if there were," said Lenny.

"Do you think they'd have blue spots?" asked Van. He'd begun to paint a dragon on one of the toilet paper rolls.

"Sure," said Lenny. He was splashing red dots on another roll.

At five-thirty the doorbell rang, four seconds after the oven timer sounded and two seconds before the dryer went off. It was Van's mother. She was wearing her nurse's uniform.

"It's lucky your mother's a nurse," said Lenny. "She can take good care of you."

Van nodded his head and smiled.

Lenny looked at his own mother with her beige gloves. He guessed they were kind of a uniform, too. Then he looked back at Van's mother, dressed in white from head to toe: white dress, white stockings, white shoes. But she didn't have gloves.

"Your friend Van doesn't look all that well," said Lenny's mother after Van had left.

"That's because he's not," said Lenny.

"I hope he doesn't have anything contagious," said

Lenny's mother. She was seated at the kitchen table, leafing through a cookbook.

"He doesn't," said Lenny. "He has a chronic illness. That's as opposed to an acute one. You know the difference?"

"Hmm," said Lenny's mother, scanning the index.

Lenny wasn't sure she was still listening. But he continued.

"Chronic illness is one that's here to stay," he said. "As long as you stay. Got it?" he asked.

"Got it," said his mother. But Lenny wasn't sure she did.

• • •

"I put a whoopee cushion under Van's seat, and he farted really loud," said Lenny.

"Was that funny?" asked Muriel.

"It was hilarious," said Lenny.

"Why?" asked Muriel.

"Nobody wants to fart," said Lenny. "It's like catching you doing something you're not supposed to. It's so dumb. Everybody farts. Mr. Ourcival farts. So does Ms. Schillinger."

"Do you fart, Lenny?"

"Sure," said Lenny. "Everyone farts. Even you, Muriel, so don't try to deny it."

"I'm not denying it," said Muriel. "Everyone farts, just like everyone cries."

"Except for me," said Lenny.

"Oh, of course," said Muriel. "Except for you."

"And my mother," said Lenny. "She doesn't cry either."

"Never?" asked Muriel.

"Didn't I tell you that?" said Lenny.

"No," said Muriel. "Maybe you just haven't seen her cry."

"Doubt it," said Lenny. "I probably get it from her."

"You know, Lenny, there's nothing wrong with crying," said Muriel.

"Babies cry," said Lenny.

"Why do you think that is?" asked Muriel.

"They're hungry," said Lenny.

"Or they feel uncomfortable inside," said Muriel. "It's the same reason that anyone cries."

"Not me," said Lenny.

13

Lenny looked at his mother. She was dressed in a red silk dress, high heels, and a pair of matching red gloves. She had a date with Bob. She'd been going out with Bob for a few months. Lenny had asked if he was her boyfriend.

"Not really," his mother had said. But Lenny wasn't sure he believed her.

"Where are you guys going?" asked Lenny.

"We're going to the movies," said his mother. She swooped down and brushed her lips across the top of Lenny's head.

The bell rang. Lenny answered the door. It was Bob.

"So how are you doing, Lenny?" asked Bob.

"I'm okay," said Lenny. He was studying Bob's shoes. They were always nicely polished. Lenny wondered if he used an electric shoe polisher, or if maybe he did it by hand.

"What are you up to, Lenny?" asked Bob.

Lenny was sorting through a pile of wires and tools on

the kitchen table. "I'm making an electrical circuit," he said.

"Well, isn't that great," said Bob.

"Sure," said Lenny. "That is, if I don't short-circuit the whole thing."

Bob looked a little worried. "Are you sure you know what you're doing?" he said.

"Sure I'm sure," said Lenny. "Look." Lenny had attached a small lightbulb to a matchbox and run wires from the base of the bulb to the ends of the box. On the ends of the box he'd attached metal clips. Lenny attached the wires to the clips, and suddenly the lightbulb lit up.

"I guess you do know what you're doing," said Bob.

"Ready," said Lenny's mother to Bob. Then she turned to Lenny. "Now, you do what Holly says," she said. Holly was the babysitter—Holly Plant. "And I've set the alarm for nine o'clock."

Most people set the alarm for waking up, but Lenny's mother set it for going to bed.

"Yup," said Lenny.

Lenny liked Holly. She was fifteen, and a neighbor. She usually spent the evening talking to her boyfriend on the phone or asking Lenny for help with her homework. She'd brought along a few math problems.

Lenny read the assignment and set to work.

"What's there to eat, Lenny?" asked Holly, heading for the kitchen.

"Air cookies," said Lenny. "On the counter. Help yourself."

Holly came back, stuffing a cookie into her mouth. "What are air cookies?" she asked.

"I put in some extra baking powder," said Lenny. "I wanted to see how high they'd rise."

"Nice, Lenny," said Holly.

"I wouldn't eat too many, though," said Lenny. "You'll fart enough to send a rocket into space."

"Gross," said Holly.

"Don't worry, Holly," said Lenny. "Everyone farts."

"Thanks, Lenny," said Holly.

• • •

"Names are funny," said Lenny. "Don't you think so, Muriel?"

"Why's that?" asked Muriel.

"Would you ever name someone Holly Plant?" said Lenny. "I mean, Holly is a plant."

"People choose names for different reasons," said Muriel. "Usually good reasons. I'm named after my great-aunt Muriel. She was my mother's favorite relative."

"Oh," said Lenny. "Do you think Lenny is a dumb name?"

"Not at all," said Muriel.

"Some people do," said Lenny.

"Some people think Muriel is a dumb name, too," said Muriel. "But you can't let that bother you, Lenny. You can't take it personally. Not everyone likes the color green, either."

"Anyone who doesn't like green is dumb," said Lenny.

"No they're not," said Muriel. "People are different and like different things."

"Well, I like green," said Lenny.

"Me too," said Muriel.

"We're alike, then," said Lenny.

"In some ways we are alike," said Muriel.

"I think my mom has a boyfriend," said Lenny. "His name is Bob."

"Do you like him?" asked Muriel.

"He's okay," said Lenny. "I don't really know him very well."

"What's he like?" asked Muriel.

"His shoes are always really shiny," said Lenny.

"What do you think that means?" asked Muriel.

"I think it means he's neat," said Lenny. "Neat like clean. Not like cool. I don't know if he's cool. I never know what to say to him."

"What does Bob do?" asked Muriel.

"You mean like for work?" asked Lenny. "I don't know."

"Do you know anything that he likes?" asked Muriel.

"He must like to play baseball," said Lenny. "He has a Reds cap and two Reds T-shirts."

"Maybe you could try talking to him about baseball," said Muriel.

"My mom smiles a lot when Bob's around," said Lenny.

"Does she smile a lot when you're around?" asked Muriel.

"Not really," said Lenny.

"Does that bother you?"

"No," said Lenny.

"Are you sure?" said Muriel.

"I guess a little bit," said Lenny. "Maybe it means she likes being with Bob more than being with me."

"I don't think it means that," said Muriel. "Do you smile a lot when she's around?"

"I don't know," said Lenny. "I never checked with myself."

• • •

"Why did you name me Lenny?" Lenny asked his mother. She was opening a new mixer. Bob had given it to her. He'd won it for being the 10,000th customer to enter the appliance store.

"Can I take apart the old one?" asked Lenny. "I need the spare parts."

"Not now, Lenny," said his mother. She tried out the different speeds of the mixer. There were five of them in all.

"Why did you name me Lenny?" Lenny asked again. "Am I named after anyone important?"

"Not really," said his mother.

"You sure?" asked Lenny.

"Yes," said his mother. "You were named after your father. His name was Lenny. If I'd known he was going to leave, I would have named you Charlie."

Lenny couldn't imagine being named Charlie. "I don't like that name," he said.

"Then you got lucky because you were already named before he took off," said Lenny's mother.

"You mean into space," said Lenny.

"Or wherever he went," said his mother. "Looking for bigger and better things."

Lenny sighed. He didn't like the name Charlie. But neither did he like being named after anyone who left his wife and baby and went into space in search of bigger and better things.

14

On Thursday, Lenny went to Van's house. This time he went directly, bypassing the playground.

"I'll pick you up in an hour," said his mother. She was taking Mrs. Ashe to the supermarket again. "Don't make me wait."

Van's mother answered the door. Her mouth was stretched into a big smile. She must be the happiest woman on earth, thought Lenny.

Van was watching television.

"Is that Dexter the scientist?" asked Lenny.

Van nodded. "I love Dexter," he said.

"Me too," said Lenny, plopping down onto the carpet.

Lenny looked at his watch.

"At four twenty-two my mother's on," he said. "Channel seven. She's advertising Plus dishwashing liquid. Just for thirty seconds. It costs too much to get a full minute of advertising time."

Van was impressed. He jumped up and grabbed the

remote control. Then he switched the channel to 7. "Let's watch it," he said.

"There's still a couple minutes to go," said Lenny.

At exactly 4:22 a pale white hand appeared on the screen. It had long fingers with manicured nails. It was holding a plate, then a bottle of dishwashing liquid. The hand went under the soap bubbles, then reemerged.

Lenny strained to get a good look at it for the brief time that it dominated the screen. It was the best look he'd ever gotten. It was undeniable. His mother had a perfect hand. That made Lenny feel good.

"That's really neat," said Van. "You must be proud of her."

"I guess I am," said Lenny, though he'd never really thought about it. He supposed he was a little proud of her. But he pushed that thought from his head.

"Now we can go back to Dexter," he said.

• • •

Lenny spun around in his chair a couple of times. Then he walked over to the shelf of objects. He picked up a seashell and held it to his ear.

"Would you like to put that shell in your space, Lenny?" asked Muriel.

"No," said Lenny. "I was just listening to the sound it makes. I bet you think it's the ocean, Muriel."

"People say it is," said Muriel.

"It's not, though," said Lenny. "It's the sound of a vacuum, and I don't mean a vacuum cleaner. I mean nothing. This is the sound of nothing."

"Do you like the sound of nothing, Lenny?" asked Muriel.

"Yup," said Lenny.

"It's kind of like the sound of quiet," said Muriel.

"Quiet is loud," said Lenny, holding the shell to his ear again. "Isn't it weird that quiet makes such a big noise."

"It is," said Muriel.

Lenny put the shell back on the shelf. He picked up a small plastic mirror and smiled at himself.

"What are you thinking about, Lenny?" asked Muriel.

"I'm thinking how happy Van's parents are. They're always smiling. Why are they so happy when Van is sick? I think they ought to be sad."

"Are you sad, Lenny?" asked Muriel.

"Yes," said Lenny.

"I'm sure Van's parents are sad, too," said Muriel. "Heartbroken even. But I bet they're putting up a good front—trying to be happy so Van will be happy. I think it would be hard for Van if his parents went around with a frown all the time. Don't you?"

"I guess so," said Lenny.

15

On Saturday, Lenny's mother decided to clean out the kitchen cupboards. They'd been invaded by legions of small black ants. A column of them was climbing up a bottle of Plus dishwashing liquid.

"Who cares about a few ants," said Lenny.

"I do," said his mother. She wasn't smiling. That made Lenny realize how much she did care.

"Want me to help?" asked Lenny.

"If you'd like," said his mother.

Lenny began taking things from the shelf and setting them on the table.

"Why don't you smile more around me?" asked Lenny.

"Do I not smile around you?" said Lenny's mother. She looked surprised.

"Not much," said Lenny.

Lenny's mother stopped what she was doing.

"I think we ought to smile more," said Lenny. "Smiling makes you happy."

"Okay," said Lenny's mother, going back to work.

Lenny followed a trail of ants down the side of the cupboard and onto the floor tiles.

"I bet if we made a trail of crumbs, we could lead them right out the door," he said.

"You do?" said his mother. Now she was smiling.

"Yup," said Lenny, smiling back.

The next day, Bob came over to help Lenny's mother in the garden. He was wearing sneakers, clean canvas ones. And he had on his Reds cap.

Bob took a seat across from Lenny at the kitchen table. "Everything okay?" he asked Lenny.

"Yup," said Lenny. He was washing his pennies in ketchup. The ketchup was acid, and the acid ate away at the dirt and left the pennies shining.

"Just think what that does to your stomach," said Bob.

"Nothing," said Lenny. "The acid is so strong in your stomach it could burn a hole in your shoes."

"The pennies look nice," said Bob. "Are you going to save them or spend them?"

"I don't know yet," said Lenny. "I haven't decided."

Bob was silent.

"What do you do for work?" asked Lenny.

"I'm in the plastics business," said Bob.

"Oh," said Lenny. "That's nice."

"I deal in Plexiglas," said Bob. "Do you know what that is?"

"Sure," said Lenny. "It's transparent, weather-resistant plastic."

"That's right," said Bob.

"Sometimes they use it in baseball fields," said Lenny. "So the ball doesn't go into the stands. I guess you'd know that because you must be a baseball fan."

"Not really," said Bob.

"Oh," said Lenny. He wasn't really sure where to go next with the conversation.

"If you're talking about my cap, then I guess I've misrepresented myself," said Bob. "I can't really get into baseball. It's too slow."

"I'll say," said Lenny. He didn't care much for baseball either.

"It's not really my kind of game," said Bob. "I'm more of a hoops man."

"Me too," said Lenny. He reeled off a slew of statistics.

"Where do you keep all those?" asked Bob.

Lenny pointed to his head. "It took me a while to memorize them." It had taken Lenny exactly three minutes.

Lenny's mother came into the kitchen. She made a pot of coffee. Bob was a coffee drinker. Lenny listened as the percolator began popping and bubbling.

"I don't like coffee," said Lenny.

"I think it's an acquired taste," said Bob. "You know, something you get used to in time."

"Hmm," said Lenny. He wondered if Bob might be like that. An acquired taste.

"Maybe we can have a game of hoops sometime," said Bob. "You know, get the blood pumping."

"Sure," said Lenny. He smiled, and Bob smiled back.

Lenny stood in the driveway bouncing a ball. He'd invited Van over.

"I think we ought to play some basketball," he said. "You know, to get the blood pumping." Lenny liked that expression.

"Okay," said Van, "but I'm not very good."

"It doesn't matter," said Lenny. He tossed the ball to Van. Van took a shot and missed. Lenny netted three in a row. Then he missed the fourth on purpose.

"You play well," said Van.

"Thanks," said Lenny, missing the next two shots. Van scored twice.

"You're pretty good, too," said Lenny. He stopped and hugged the ball to his chest. He felt a drop of water hit his forehead and dribble down his nose.

"It's raining," said Van. "I guess we better stop."

"We don't have to," said Lenny.

"I'm a little tired," said Van.

Lenny noticed that Van was breathing hard. His cheeks were red. Lenny could see that they'd gotten the blood pumping. And that made him happy.

"Let's stop, then," he said.

They sat down on the steps under the awning and watched the rain fall. Lenny reached out his hand and caught a drop. Then he held it to his tongue. It was cold. Then he let a drop fall onto his shirt and another onto his pants.

"Look," he said. "The water expands more on my shirt than my pants. That means my shirt is more absorbent. And that means if it starts to rain hard, my shirt will get soaking wet first."

Van watched the drops hit his shirt, then his pants. "My pants are more absorbent," he said.

"I'm going to be an inventor someday," said Lenny.

"What are you going to invent?" asked Van.

"I don't know yet," said Lenny. "But now that I think of it, wouldn't it be neat if there was a special spray that you could spray on you when it rained and it would make you waterproof. Then you wouldn't need raincoats and umbrellas and you wouldn't get wet. It would be great for pets and animals."

"Their fur gets really wet," said Van. "But you'd have to be able to wash it off."

"I'd make it so you could peel it off," said Lenny. "Or maybe it could evaporate after an hour." Lenny looked up at the bright wheel of sun that was rolling out of a cloud.

"Do you think there's going to be a rainbow?" asked Van.

"If there isn't, I can make one," said Lenny.

"I don't think you can make a rainbow," said Van. "I don't mean you, I mean anyone," he added.

"I can," said Lenny, jumping to his feet. "It's easy."

"Rainbows are lucky," said Van.

He followed Lenny into the house. Lenny got his baby bathtub from the storage room and filled it with water. Then he placed it in front of the dining room window. It was still drizzling, but the sun was shining. Lenny went into the bathroom and got a mirror, one with a plastic handle.

"You can't use metal," he said. "Or else it will rust."

He put the mirror in the water, propped against the side of the bathtub. "Look," he said.

A rainbow appeared on the wall, arching over the doorway.

"That's amazing," said Van.

Lenny's mother came zipping through the dining room with the vacuum cleaner.

"Hi, Van," she said, turning the vacuum cleaner off.

"Hello, Mrs. Brewster," said Van.

"What are you two doing?" asked Lenny's mother. She looked worried.

"We're making a rainbow," said Lenny.

"Oh," said his mother. "Just put away the tub when you're finished. Okay?"

"Okay," said Lenny.

Lenny's mother pushed the button on the vacuum cleaner and set off like a freight train picking up steam.

"Your mother moves fast," said Van.

"Yeah," said Lenny. "Sometimes I think she has a battery somewhere."

Van laughed. "I wish I had a battery," he said.

• • •

"I can make a rainbow," Lenny said.

"How do you do that, Lenny?" asked Muriel.

"You just put a mirror in some water," he said. "The light from the sun bounces off the water and makes a rainbow somewhere in the room. It depends on the angle of reflection."

"I'm going to try that sometime," said Muriel. "I love rainbows."

"Van says rainbows are lucky," said Lenny.

"I think he's right," said Muriel.

"I'd like one for my space," said Lenny. "Do you have one?"

"I don't," said Muriel. "But you can draw one."

"It's not the same," said Lenny.

Lenny walked over to the shelf of objects. He picked

up a small clear plastic cube and turned it over in his hand. Then he picked up a miniature basketball and set it in his space.

"Do you like to play basketball, Muriel?" he asked.

"Not really," said Muriel. "I was never very good at ball sports."

"That's okay," said Lenny. "I bet you're good at a lot of other things."

"Thank you, Lenny, for reminding me of that," said Muriel.

16

Lenny met Van at the playground. They took a couple of trips each down the slide, then they sat on the bench next to the swings. Van opened his backpack and pulled out his robot. "It's breaking down," he said. "I don't know what's wrong with it. It was okay up until yesterday."

Lenny took the robot and turned it upside down. "It's made in China," he said. "That's what's wrong with it. Cheap parts. If my mother would let me take apart her old mixer, I could probably fix it."

Van and Lenny walked toward Van's house. Van wanted to show Lenny his dragons.

"I don't really like dragons," said Lenny.

"I made these ones," said Van. "I painted them."

He led Lenny down the hallway. Audrey was in her crib, gurgling in her sleep. Suddenly she burst out crying.

"Maybe she had a bad dream," said Lenny.

"She probably just passed some gas," said Van.

"Oh yeah," said Lenny. "I forgot. Babies fart a lot."

Van's father picked up Audrey and patted her on the

back. Lenny reached his hand out and tickled her feet. Audrey stopped crying and looked at him.

"She likes that," said Van.

"Thank you, Lenny," said Mr. James.

"Anytime," said Lenny. He gave Audrey one last tickle.

Van stopped by the table outside his bedroom door. He crushed a couple of pills and washed them down. Then he showed Lenny a small electronic device attached to a wristband.

"It's for taking blood pressure," said Van. He slid the cuff onto Lenny's arm. Then he watched the numbers register in a small plastic window.

"Am I okay?" asked Lenny.

"Perfect," said Van. Lenny picked up a syringe and pretended to give the robot a shot. Van laughed.

Lenny followed Van to his room.

"Here they are," said Van. Across the floor was a carpet of colorful dragons, some with claws and bulging eyes, others with stripes and spots. And they were all smiling.

Lenny smiled, too. "These are really nice," he said.

"You can have one, if you want," said Van.

"Really?" said Lenny.

"Sure," said Van. "Pick one."

Lenny studied the dragons, flying, sitting, sleeping.

He finally chose one swooping downward with out-stretched arms. It was green, yellow, and red, like the flag of Senegal.

"I like this one," he said.

"That one wards off evil," said Van.

Van took the dragon and rolled it up. Then he slipped a rubber band around it.

"Do you want to draw something?" Van asked.

"Maybe a rainbow," said Lenny. "A really small one."

Van got down on his hands and knees and drew an arc. Then Lenny began coloring in the rays of light—red, orange, yellow, green, blue, indigo, violet. When they were finished, Van cut the rainbow out and handed it to Lenny.

"Thanks," said Lenny.

• • •

Lenny didn't sit down. He walked right up to his space.

"Can I put tape on the shelf?" asked Lenny.

"Yes," said Muriel.

"Do you have any?" asked Lenny.

Muriel reached into her desk drawer and pulled out a roll of Scotch tape. She handed it to Lenny.

Lenny took the rainbow that he and Van had painted, and stuck it to the back wall of his space.

"Van and I made it," said Lenny.

"It's beautiful," said Muriel.

Lenny traced the blue line with his index finger. Then he sat back in his chair. He took a spin, then faced Muriel.

"Rainbows are lucky," he reminded Muriel.

"Did I tell you that Van has a table outside his door with all kinds of medicine and shots?" said Lenny. "He has a pill crusher. Did you ever see one of those?"

"I don't think I have," said Muriel.

"You put the pill in and press down and it crushes it into powder so you can swallow it easier," said Lenny.

"Sounds like a great invention," said Muriel.

"I wish I'd invented it," said Lenny.

"There'll be other things for you to invent," said Muriel.

"Van took my blood pressure," said Lenny.

"Really?" said Muriel. "He can do that?"

"Yup," said Lenny. "And it was good."

"I'm glad to hear that," said Muriel.

"I think he's pretty brave," said Lenny.

"Why is that?" said Muriel.

"All those pills and shots he has to have," said Lenny. "I hate shots and I hate taking pills. I think Van must hate it, too. But he has to do it if he wants to get better."

"Sometimes just knowing we have to do something

gives us courage," said Muriel. "Anyway, I think it's wonderful that you think Van is brave."

"I really like him," said Lenny.

"It sounds like he likes you, too," said Muriel.

"I hope so," said Lenny.

"Muriel, do you like dragons?" asked Lenny.

"I don't know any," said Muriel. "What about you?"

"I hate the kind that everyone here at school has. The kind with poisoned spit and double-edged claws," said Lenny. "They're mean and scary."

"I don't think I'd like those either," said Muriel.

"Van made some dragons," said Lenny. "They're really nice colors, and they're all smiling. He gave me one that wards off evil. If you want to see it, I'll bring it to show you."

"I'd love to see it," said Muriel.

17

Lenny finished his homework. Then he flicked on the television with the remote control and turned to the cartoons. Dexter was on. He was inventing a robot that could do everything.

"Great idea, Dex," said Lenny. "But not even a robot can do everything." Lenny hadn't really thought this through, but he knew he was right.

At 4:20, Lenny changed the channel. "Sorry, Dex," he said. He sat back and waited for the commercial to start. It was the advertisement for Plus dishwashing liquid. He'd seen it at least a dozen times, but he wanted to see it again. He watched the hand appear in the upper right-hand corner of the screen, like always. It was a strange feeling to see that hand detached from a body. Lenny wasn't sure he wanted to buy soap from a hand when he couldn't see the body. He wished he could see the body, though he knew whose it was. It was his mother's.

Lenny looked for some detail that would distinguish that hand from all the others out there in the world. It had five perfect long thin fingers with perfect nails. It was attached to a perfect wrist that turned and twisted gracefully. You couldn't see the veins with the blood flowing through them. Or the bones. The hand could actually have been that of a robot, thought Lenny. He wondered why they didn't use robot hands instead of people hands. Nobody really had a perfect hand like that. And there was no hand which could move that wasn't attached to a body.

Lenny heard the front door bang shut. It was his mother. She'd taken out the trash. It was recycling day. Taking out the trash was Lenny's job. But he'd forgotten.

"That you, Mom?" he asked. "I hope it's not a robber or something," he shouted. "Anyway, there's nothing here to take but a lot of gloves."

"Just me," said Lenny's mother, popping her head into the living room. Lenny turned. His eyes went straight to his mother's hands. He wanted to find some connection between what he'd seen on television and what he was seeing now.

• • •

"Did you ever see that cartoon *Dexter*?" Lenny asked.

"No," said Muriel.

"He's a scientist," said Lenny. "He invents stuff."

"That sounds interesting," said Muriel. "What does he invent?"

"The other day he was inventing a robot that could do everything. I don't think a robot could do everything," said Lenny. "Do you?"

"What couldn't a robot do?" asked Muriel.

"A robot couldn't really take care of a baby," said Lenny.

"Why not?" said Muriel.

"A baby needs milk," said Lenny. "A robot doesn't have milk."

"A robot could give a baby a bottle of powdered milk," said Muriel.

"Not as good as a mother could," said Lenny. "And a robot couldn't hug you or kiss you."

"Why not?" said Muriel.

"Maybe it could," said Lenny. "But it wouldn't be the same."

"That's because a robot doesn't have feelings," said Muriel. "And feelings are what makes us people. If a robot is programmed correctly, it doesn't make mistakes. That's what makes us people, too, Lenny."

"I guess a robot doesn't have that empathy thing," said Lenny.

"I think it would be hard to make a robot with empathy," said Muriel. "Even for Dexter."

"Do you ever wear gloves, Muriel?" asked Lenny.

"Sometimes on special occasions," said Muriel. "Like weddings."

"I just wear them in the winter," said Lenny.

"I wear them in the winter, too," said Muriel.

"My mother has about fifty pairs," said Lenny. "In all different colors."

"Does she collect them?" asked Muriel.

"She wears them," said Lenny. "That's because she's a hand model."

"You never told me that, Lenny," said Muriel.

"I'm telling you now," said Lenny. "She's a hand model, and I bet you've seen her a bunch of times on TV. At least, her hands."

"What exactly does she do?" asked Muriel.

"She models soap and jewelry," said Lenny. "You know that ad where you see the hand putting a plate into soapy water? That's her."

"That's fascinating," said Muriel. "I didn't even realize that hand models existed."

"Sure they do," said Lenny. "They have to get people who have perfect hands to model, otherwise no one will buy the stuff. My mother has perfect hands. Not everyone does. You got to be born with them."

"I see," said Muriel.

"And you got to take good care of them, too," said Lenny. "You have to wear gloves all the time to protect them. One broken nail and she could lose a job. No sun. No cuts or scratches. People don't like to see ugly or scarred hands. Then they don't buy the stuff."

"Being a hand model sounds like hard work," said Muriel.

"It is," said Lenny. "My mother can never touch anything, and no one can touch her."

"That must be difficult," said Muriel. "For her and everyone around her."

"You know, I might buy something anyway," said Lenny. "Even if someone had an ugly hand."

"Why is that, Lenny?" asked Muriel.

"I think the perfect hand is just a trick to get you to buy stuff," said Lenny.

"You sound angry, Lenny," said Muriel. "Does that make you mad?"

"Yes," said Lenny.

"Why?" asked Muriel.

"If my mother was selling soap with imperfect hands, I'd buy it anyway," said Lenny.

"That's because she's your mother, Lenny," said Muriel.

"I wish she didn't have to wear those gloves all the time," said Lenny.

"Does she ever take them off?" said Muriel.

"Hardly ever," said Lenny. "Then it's just for a few minutes. Sometimes she sleeps without them. So her skin can breathe. Did you know that skin breathed, Muriel?"

"I did," said Muriel.

"Can you see my skin breathing, Muriel?" asked Lenny.

"I can't," said Muriel. "But lots of things are going on in our bodies all the time that we can't see. Lots of good things."

18

Van peered into the aquarium on the kitchen counter in Lenny's house. He watched the fish dart in and out of a small coral arch. Their tails made tiny currents in the water.

"Did you notice I'm losing my hair?" he said quietly. "It's the medicine I'm taking. It's a new kind."

Lenny looked at Van. He hadn't noticed. "It's okay," he said. "I still think you look really great."

"It's going to grow back," said Van.

"Even if it didn't, you'd still look good," said Lenny.

"Do you think so?" asked Van.

"Do I think so?" Lenny repeated. "I know so."

"Some of that medicine makes me feel sick," said Van. "But I have to get sick to get better. That's strange, isn't it?"

"Well," said Lenny, "I guess the world is like that. You have to go up to go down. You have to go in to go out. That's just how it is."

Lenny was remembering what Muriel had said about

Van's parents putting up a good front. He wanted to put up a good front, too.

"I like your fish," said Van.

"I wanted a dog," said Lenny. "But my mother said dogs are too much work. So it's fish or nothing."

"I like fish," said Van.

"Me too," said Lenny. "But they're kind of hard to play with. You can't really teach them to roll over or fetch."

Lenny took Van to his room. "What do you want to do?" he asked. "We can do anything you want."

"Did you finish painting the toilet paper rolls?" asked Van. "We could start making the tower."

"Okay," said Lenny. "But we have to do it in modules."

"What are modules?" asked Van.

"Modules are like little units," said Lenny. "That way we can assemble it and reassemble it. Otherwise we'll never get it out of my room."

"Okay," said Van.

• • •

"You have hair on your sweater, Muriel," said Lenny.

"So I do," said Muriel. "I seem to be shedding. I guess it's that time of year."

"Did you know that the hairs that fall are already six years old?" said Lenny.

"Is that so?" said Muriel.

"Yup," said Lenny. "No hair lasts more than six years."

"I didn't know that," said Muriel. "You are just a wealth of information, Lenny."

"Anyway, you lose about a hundred per day," said Lenny. "Unless you're sick, and then you lose more."

"What do you mean?" asked Muriel.

"Like Van. He's losing a lot of hair. More like a couple hundred a day, I'd say," said Lenny. "That's because of the medicine he's taking to make him better."

"I see," said Muriel. "Those must be some of the side effects. But it's worth it if Van gets better."

"His hair will grow back when he stops taking the medicine," said Lenny. "Anyway, I like him with hair or without."

"Good for you," said Muriel.

"I wonder if he'd like me without hair," said Lenny.

"I'm sure he would," said Muriel.

"I guess hair isn't so important," said Lenny.

"I guess not," said Muriel.

"Do you think you'd like me without hair, Muriel?" said Lenny.

"I know I would," said Muriel.

19

"I'm sorry, Lenny," said Mrs. James. "Van's not going to be able to make it today." Lenny had made a date with Van to go to the playground after school.

"It's just to take a couple of rides down the slide," said Lenny.

"I know," said Mrs. James. "But Van is tired today and he's taking a nap."

"He's okay, isn't he?" asked Lenny.

"Oh yes," said Mrs. James. "Why don't you come by tomorrow, Lenny."

Lenny stopped by the next day. Van came to the door. He looked pale to Lenny.

"I don't feel too much like sliding," he said. "I don't really feel like going out."

"Oh," said Lenny. He didn't know what else to say. He noticed Van had lost more of his hair. "You look good," he added.

"Thanks," said Van.

Lenny strolled back across the street toward the playground. "Tired," he said. "I'm tired, too."

Suddenly Lenny felt tired of school, tired of sliding, tired of everything.

At recess the next day, Lenny asked to go to the library. "I have to look up something," he said to Ms. Schillinger. "It's really important."

Ms. Schillinger sighed, but she let Lenny go. "All right, Lenny," she said.

Lenny went straight up to Mrs. Marsh. "I need a book on diseases," he said.

"What kind of diseases?" asked Mrs. Marsh. "There are lots of them, you know."

"Chronic blood ones," said Lenny.

"Any one in particular?" asked Mrs. Marsh.

"Leukemia," said Lenny.

Mrs. Marsh's eyebrows shot up. "Okay, Lenny," she said. "That sounds serious."

She steered Lenny down an aisle and began pulling books off the shelf. "How about this one?" she said, handing a small volume to Lenny. It had photographs.

Lenny opened the book and began to read aloud. " 'Leukemia is any of various acute or chronic neoplastic diseases of the bone marrow in which there is unrestrained proliferation of white blood cells.' "

Lenny turned the page. There were lots of pictures of white blood cells duplicating and banging into one another.

"Crash, clash," said Lenny out loud.

"Shh, Lenny," said Mrs. Marsh.

Lenny kept reading. " 'This leads to infection, shortage of red blood cells, and other disorders, and can often be fatal.' "

Lenny looked back at the photo of the cells crashing into one another. He suddenly felt as if he might explode. He didn't bother to take a deep breath. Suddenly Lenny couldn't contain himself any longer.

"BANG!" he shouted, ramming his fist into the sick cells on the page. "That'll teach you not to take over."

"I'm going to have to ask you to leave the library, Lenny," said Mrs. Marsh.

Mr. Ourcival was in the back room making coffee. Decaf. He only drank decaf, and he let everyone know that. Lenny leaned back on two legs of the small wooden chair, trying to balance himself.

"Long time no see, Lenny," said Mr. Ourcival. He was stirring his coffee with a pencil.

"Did you miss me?" asked Lenny.

Mr. Ourcival answered Lenny's question with one of his own.

"Did you not realize the library was a place for quiet?"

he said. "You're a smart boy, Lenny. Smart enough to know that by now. I don't know what it's going to take to teach you that there's a time and place for everything."

But Mr. Ourcival did seem to know what it might take. For the rest of the week, Lenny spent recess time folding milk cartons for recycling. He folded each into a different shape. He liked the feel of the wax coating. It was fun. He didn't think about the library. Or Van. He thought only about whether or not the object he was creating should have wings or be streamlined. Then he thought how he would like to squish Mr. Ourcival into one of those cartons and launch him on a reconnaissance mission into space.

"If it's not in the dirty clothes basket, it doesn't get washed," said Lenny's mother. Lenny had left his clothes right where he stepped out of them—beside the two other piles from the previous two days. He hadn't made his bed either.

"I'm not making your bed for you," said Lenny's mother. "I thought we'd gotten past that. You were doing so well. What's wrong with you, Lenny? Now you're going backward."

"Don't you know?" said Lenny. "You have to go back to go forward. You have to get sicker to get better. It's a law. Just like gravity."

"What?" said his mother.

"Nothing," said Lenny.

● ● ●

"Lenny, what were you doing in Mr. Ourcival's office?" asked Muriel. "Did the breathing not work?"

"I was in the library," said Lenny. "I was reading a really scary book."

"Do you want to tell me about it?" asked Muriel.

"Not really," said Lenny.

"What's wrong, Lenny?" asked Muriel.

"I don't know," said Lenny. "I'm tired. Don't you ever get tired?"

"Yes," said Muriel. "I think everyone gets tired. But are you just tired, Lenny?"

"Being tired makes me mad," said Lenny.

"Why do you think that is?" asked Muriel.

"Wouldn't it be great if people never got sick," said Lenny. "And they never died."

"Then we'd never be sad," said Muriel. "And we wouldn't make others sad."

"And no one would get mad," said Lenny.

"And no one would have to take those deep breaths," said Muriel.

"No one would have to take any breath at all," said Lenny.

"And if no one breathed?" said Muriel.

"Then we wouldn't be alive," said Lenny.

"That's right, Lenny," said Muriel.

Lenny went over to his space. He wanted to add something, but he wasn't sure what. At last he chose an acorn. It looked like a little round head with a hat.

"This is all dried up," he said to Muriel. "See how light it is?"

Lenny put the acorn next to the Mexican jumping bean.

"Acorns grow to be big oak trees," he said.

"I know," said Muriel.

"This won't grow, though, because no one's planted it," said Lenny.

"Not all acorns grow into big trees," said Muriel. "That's just the way of life."

20

"Did you ever think about what you might like to do when you grow up?" said Muriel.

"I don't think I want to grow up," said Lenny.

"Why don't you want to grow up, Lenny?" asked Muriel.

"I don't know," said Lenny.

"Think about it," said Muriel.

"Grownup people do bad things," said Lenny.

"Like what?" asked Muriel.

"They just get up and leave," said Lenny.

"Are you talking about your father, Lenny?" said Muriel. "Did he just get up and leave?"

"He did," said Lenny.

"What your father did, Lenny, wasn't really a very grownup thing to do," said Muriel. "But sometimes it's hard even for grownups to be grownup."

"They shoot into space and they never come back again," said Lenny. "Once you're in space—that really outer part—you can't come back."

"Things change, Lenny," said Muriel. "Maybe someday people will be able to go into space and come back. Maybe someday someone will discover a cure for Van's illness that doesn't make him tired or make him lose his hair. Things change, Lenny. We change."

"We grow up and someday we die," said Lenny.

"Yes," said Muriel. "There's no life without death, Lenny."

"I don't like to think of dying," said Lenny. "It's scary."

"It's scary for everyone, Lenny," said Muriel. "But death is just another change."

21

"Do you want to go to the playground tomorrow?" Lenny asked. He'd telephoned Van.

"I don't think so," said Van. "I have a cold. My ear aches."

"Oh," said Lenny. "Too bad."

"It's all right," said Van. "I'll be okay in a few days."

Instead, Lenny went to the supermarket with his mother and Mrs. Ashe. He started down the cereal aisle, stopping to count the number of different choices. There were eighty-seven in all. Lenny took a box of Cheerios and dropped them into his mother's shopping cart. Then he moved on. Mrs. Ashe was leaning over the smoked salmon, checking the expiration dates. She had to put on her glasses to read them.

Lenny bent down and looked under the shelves. He usually managed to find some coins abandoned in the aisles or near the checkout lanes. Lenny reached under the chip rack and pulled out a quarter. He found a nickel in the canned goods section.

Lenny studied the faces of his coins. He liked dimes the best. He wondered who decided whose faces to put on the coins. He imagined his own face on one. Then he put the money in his pants pocket. He was dressed like the Swedish flag—yellow and blue.

Lenny met his mother at the checkout counter. Mrs. Ashe was unloading her shopping cart. She always bought the same things: smoked salmon, a couple of chocolate bars, some vanilla wafers, and pineapple juice. Lenny wondered if all old people ate the same things.

Lenny looked at the machine that spit back change. Beside it was a collection box for MS.

"What's MS?" Lenny asked his mother.

"Multiple sclerosis," said his mother. "It's a disease."

" 'The crippler of young adults,' " read Lenny. "How young? Like your age?"

"Sometimes," said his mother. She was taking things out of her cart and piling them onto the conveyer belt. She was wearing her leather gloves, the ones she always wore when she shopped.

Usually Lenny would linger at the checkout and buy a pack of gum or something else with the coins he'd found. But Lenny looked at the box in front of him. It was pleading for help. HELP was written in big letters across one of its sides.

"Help," said Lenny, a little too loudly. A few people looked at him. The checkout girl rolled her eyes. Lenny

watched her pass each item over a small glass screen set into the conveyer belt.

"How does that thing work?" asked Lenny. "How does that machine know what those things cost?"

"Beats me," said the girl.

Lenny peered into the glass to get a better look.

"Better watch it," said the girl. "It scans anything that passes over it."

"Lenny," said his mother.

Lenny straightened up. He surveyed the varieties of chewing gum stacked on the rack beside the checkout counter. He thought how strange it was that chewing gum came in different shapes and sizes. It came in strips and in squares, like Chiclets. Sometimes you could even find little round balls of gum. Suddenly Lenny found himself wondering why no one had invented rainbow gum—long strips with seven different colors and flavors merged together in a rainbow pattern. If you chewed it you'd be lucky. Lenny smiled at the thought.

Then his mind turned to Muriel. She liked chewing gum. She always had a load of it. He was thinking of buying her some. Blueberry maybe. He bet it would turn her tongue blue. He thought how he'd like to see that. But then he changed his mind. He took the thirty cents from his pocket and dropped it into the box asking for help.

• • •

"I was going to buy you some gum the other day," said Lenny. "It was blueberry. I bet you don't have any of that."

"I don't," said Muriel. "That was thoughtful of you, Lenny."

"Anyway, I changed my mind," said Lenny. "I thought it might turn your tongue blue. So I gave my money to some people who needed help."

"That was nice of you, Lenny," said Muriel.

"Are you mad at me?" asked Lenny.

"No," said Muriel. "There's no reason to be."

"You know gum is bad for your teeth anyway," said Lenny. "Too much sugar. Unless it's the sugarless kind, and that's not as good."

"I know," said Muriel.

"Do you know what MS is?" asked Lenny.

"Yes," said Muriel. "It's a disease of the nervous system."

"Young adults get it," said Lenny.

"That's right," said Muriel.

"You don't have it or anything, do you?" asked Lenny.

"No," said Muriel.

"Good," said Lenny. "Because you know it can cripple you."

"I know," said Muriel.

Lenny got up and walked over to his space. He clapped his hands and set the jumping bean in motion.

Then he picked up the rubber man and bent his legs backward and forward. He turned on the key to the windup clown. Pretty soon everything was in motion.

"I guess none of these guys have MS either," said Lenny. Then he spun around a couple of times before returning to his chair.

"I'm going to invent a new kind of gum," said Lenny. "Rainbow gum."

"What's it going to be like?" asked Muriel.

"It's going to be these long strips of gum with seven flavors and colors mixed together in stripes."

"It sounds delicious," said Muriel.

"And when you chew it, you get lucky," said Lenny.

"I can't wait," said Muriel.

"Well, you're going to have to," said Lenny. "It's going to take some time."

"I'll try to be patient," said Muriel.

"Someday I'm going to invent a device to trap germs, too," said Lenny. "Then no one would ever get sick. No earaches. There wouldn't be any MS or any leukemia. Or any of those other terrible things that people get. Good people, by the way. Wouldn't that be great?" said Lenny. "Then people would only die of old age."

"It would be," said Muriel. "There might be a problem with room, though. It might get pretty crowded."

"By then we'll have discovered space and we'll be moving in and out of it," said Lenny. "In our spacecraft."

"And you might find your father," said Muriel.

"Or he might find me," said Lenny.

"I wonder what we'd do for food?" said Muriel.

"All that will have changed," said Lenny. "We probably wouldn't have to grow food or anything. It would be made in a laboratory. And we'd be buying it in small packs like gum. We might even be able to chew it like gum and it wouldn't rot our teeth."

"I hope there'd still be real gum," said Muriel.

"Don't worry," said Lenny. "There'll probably be something better than gum."

"You're probably right," said Muriel.

"You know those little boxes that they have sometimes in the supermarket? Where they collect money for diseases?" asked Lenny.

"Yes," said Muriel.

"Where do you think that money goes?" asked Lenny.

"It goes to research organizations," said Muriel. "To people like you, Lenny, who hope to find cures."

22

Lenny stood on the doorstep of his house. His mother rummaged through her purse, looking for her keys. Lenny rang the doorbell even though he knew no one was home.

"Why are you ringing the bell?" asked his mother.

"I like it," said Lenny. He liked the sound it made. It was a buzzer-like noise that reverberated through his whole body like a mini electric shock.

Lenny's mother unlocked the door. Lenny rushed by her into the kitchen.

"Do you want me to make you a snack?" asked his mother.

"I'm not really hungry," said Lenny.

He opened a drawer and got a pair of scissors and some Scotch tape. Then he found a sheet of cardboard and went to his room. He cut the cardboard into squares and folded them to make a box. Then he cut a slot in the top of it large enough for a big coin and painted the box green. He took a blue marker and wrote the word HELP on one of the sides. On another he drew a face with a smile. It looked like a little acorn. Then on another side he wrote: WIPE OUT LEUKEMIA.

The next day Lenny took his box to school. He put it on the corner of his desk, but no one seemed to notice it. At recess Lenny took his box out to the playground. He stood at the bottom of the slide. The slide was the most popular piece of playground equipment. It attracted a lot of kids.

"What's in the box?" asked Will.

"I'm collecting money to wipe out a disease," said Lenny. "Want to give some?"

"How do I know you're telling the truth?" said Will.

"Because I am," said Lenny.

"But you're weird," said Will.

Then someone told Ms. Schillinger that Lenny was collecting money to buy himself a new skateboard.

Lenny ended up in Mr. Ourcival's office with his money box. He held it up to the principal.

"Want to give something?" Lenny asked. "It's for a good cause. It's to research a cure for leukemia. You know what that is, don't you?"

"Yes, I do, Lenny," said Mr. Ourcival. "It's a blood disease. But you can't just go around collecting money for causes. You need permission to do that. That's not official,

Lenny. You need a license and an organization to back you up and see that the funds are spent properly. How do I know you're not collecting money for something else?"

"Because I'm telling you I'm not," said Lenny. His face fell.

"Some people might think you are," said Mr. Ourcival. "There are people who do things like that."

"Stupid people," said Lenny.

"Perhaps," said Mr. Ourcival. He leaned back in his chair. It was the first time Lenny had seen him do that. Mr. Ourcival stretched. "It's a good thought, Lenny," he said. "But that's not how it's done."

Lenny waited for a punishment, but there was none. Mr. Ourcival ushered him to the door and sent him back to class. He even managed to smile.

Lenny stood in the hallway looking at his box. He wanted to drop it on the floor and turn it into a two-dimensional object. But then he saw the little acorn face smiling up at him, and he changed his mind.

• • •

"What have you got, Lenny?" asked Muriel.

"A box," said Lenny. "An unofficial one."

"What's it for?" asked Muriel.

"I made it to collect money for leukemia," said Lenny. "To help find a cure. You know, like those boxes they have at the supermarket. But Mr. Ourcival says it's not official. He says I need permission to collect money. It's like you need permission to be nice."

"It's not exactly like that, Lenny," said Muriel. "There are organizations that act as sponsors and take care of money that's collected. Otherwise, what would you do with it? You have to make sure it gets into the right hands."

"I could take it to the hospital," said Lenny.

"It's more complicated than that, Lenny," said Muriel. "Maybe we can look into those organizations and see if we can get an official box for the school."

"Okay," said Lenny. "You want this box?"

"I'd love that box," said Muriel. "Even if it is un-official. That was a very thoughtful thing that you did, Lenny. I'm proud of you. I'm sure Van would be, too."

"Do you think I'm weird?" Lenny asked.

"Not at all," said Muriel. "Do you think you're weird?"

"Not really," said Lenny.

"Good," said Muriel.

23

Margery stood at the entrance of the school with a box. She had an official box from the American Cancer Society—a collection box for leukemia. Lenny watched the boys and girls pass and drop coins into the slot carved in the top.

"Hey, where'd you get that box?" asked Lenny.

"My mom got it where she works," said Margery. "I have permission to do this," she said. She pointed to a badge that she'd pinned to her chest.

Lenny swallowed hard. He listened to the coins drop into the box. It was a metal box, not cardboard, and you could hear a plink plink as the money hit the bottom. Lenny liked that sound.

Lenny stood back. He took several very deep breaths. He felt like a fire-breathing dragon. He hated Margery.

"Your mother named you for stale margarine," he said. "That's just cheap butter. You live up to your name."

No one was listening, not even Margery. Lenny lingered for a while watching. At last he reached his hands into his pockets. He'd put on his camping shorts even though it was still chilly. In one of the back pockets he had twenty quarters, which made him look like he had a load in his pants. He jingled them for a few seconds that seemed like hours. He thought about hurling them into the air and letting them fall randomly where they might. But then he wandered up to Margery. He didn't look at her face. He hated that face. He took his quarters, one by one, and dropped them into the metal box. They each went plink.

Margery sighed after the fifth. The bell rang for class.

"We're going to be late," said Margery.

"Not done," said Lenny. He kept dropping the quarters in slowly.

"Hurry up," shouted Margery.

Lenny looked at Margery. He had an urge to stuff the quarters into her mouth. But if he did that, he knew they wouldn't end up at the American Cancer Society. They'd end up in the toilet. And that wouldn't help Van.

"Are you done?" asked Margery.

"Think so," said Lenny. He reached into each of his other six pockets. He took out several lint balls, a pack of Kleenex, a couple of marbles, and a pack of crackers. He still had the urge to fill the bottomless pit that was Margery's mouth.

"Want a cracker?" he asked.

"No," said Margery.

Lenny spent the morning making a mental note of defects in the classroom. He only needed about 20 percent of his brain to do his schoolwork, so he had 80 percent left to concentrate on peeling paint and other things. He thought the clock needed a new battery. He was sure it was starting to lose tenths of a second. Many of the chairs were chipped, and some had deep carvings that looked like scars. There were desks that had lost paint. A lightbulb needed replacing in one of the ceiling lamps, which gave off too much heat as far as Lenny was concerned. Ms. Schillinger had a run in her stockings. Then there was Margery. She was a defect. The world was full of defects. That thought bothered Lenny.

• • •

"There's a bunch of things that need fixing here," said Lenny.

"I know," said Muriel.

"I think your doorknob's going to fall off," said Lenny. "The carpet stinks. This electric wiring could cause a major meltdown any minute. The wattage in your lightbulb is too high, Muriel."

"Do you want to tell me what's wrong, Lenny?" asked Muriel.

"What's wrong?" repeated Lenny. "Apart from everything I just mentioned, Margery got an official box and she's collecting money. She even has a badge which says American Cancer Society."

"I'm sorry, Lenny," said Muriel. "That would make me mad, too."

"She got it just because she knows the right people," said Lenny. "I know the right people, too. I know Van. He's the right one."

"I agree, Lenny," said Muriel. "I know exactly how you feel."

"Now everyone thinks Margery is great and wonderful," said Lenny.

"Everyone except you," said Muriel. "What do you think?"

"I think she's a big fat cow. She doesn't really care about Van. She just cares about herself. I hate her."

"I know you do," said Muriel. "And that's okay. But let's look on the bright side. She collected some money for the disease. And she's going to have to turn it over to the American Cancer Society because she has an official box. Even if she did it for herself, it's going to help Van."

"I wasn't doing it for myself," said Lenny.

"I know you weren't, Lenny," said Muriel. "Did you give Margery any money?"

"Twenty big Georgie Porgies," said Lenny.

"Georgie Porgies?" said Muriel.

"Quarters," said Lenny. "George Washington's on them."

"That's five dollars," said Muriel. "That was generous of you, Lenny."

24

On Thursday, Lenny showed up on Van's doorstep.

"Surprise!" he said.

"Hi," said Van, smiling. He was feeling better. He looked a little less tired.

"What are you doing?" asked Lenny.

"Packing," said Van. He led Lenny up the stairs and to his bedroom. A suitcase lay open on the foot of his bed. "I'm going away next week," he said.

"Where?" asked Lenny.

"Minneapolis," said Van. "I'm going to get an operation to fix me for good."

"That's great," said Lenny, wondering if Margery's collection had already found its way into the right hands.

"How long are you going for?" asked Lenny.

"Just about a week," said Van.

"And when you come back you're going to be perfect," said Lenny.

"No one's perfect," said Van.

"Well, you're going to be pretty close," said Lenny.

"I hope so," said Van.

"Are you scared?" asked Lenny.

"Not really," said Van. "They're going to put me to sleep, so I guess it will be okay."

Lenny was caught off guard. He wished he had something to give to Van for his trip.

"Hey, we didn't finish our tower," he said. "Maybe you should collect any toilet paper rolls you find there. Sort of as a souvenir. We can finish the tower when you get back."

"Will do," said Van.

Lenny handed Van his pajamas and socks. He watched Van stack everything neatly in his small suitcase and close the lid.

"I know it's just for a week," said Lenny. "But I'll miss you."

"Me too," said Van. "But I'll be back before you know it."

• • •

"Van's gone," said Lenny. "To Minneapolis."

"Why's that?" asked Muriel.

"He's going to get a bone marrow transplant so he can make his own blood cells," said Lenny.

"That's great news," said Muriel.

"I'm really happy for him," said Lenny.

"Me too," said Muriel.

"He's not even scared," said Lenny. "I'd be scared if I was going to have an operation and they were going to have to cut me open."

"He sounds like a pretty brave guy," said Muriel.

"He is brave," said Lenny. "I'm going to think about him a lot."

"I think that's a good idea," said Muriel. "I think it can really help a person. I'm going to think about him, too."

"You don't even know him," said Lenny.

"I do," said Muriel. "At least, I feel like I know him, thanks to you, Lenny. I wish I did know him."

"I can introduce you when he gets back," said Lenny.

"I'll look forward to that," said Muriel. "I think Van's lucky to have a friend like you, Lenny."

"You do?" said Lenny.

"I do," said Muriel.

• • •

Lenny counted off the days that Van would be gone. He had a dartboard calendar he'd made from a sheet of Styrofoam. Every day that passed, he threw a dart. Usually he forgot some and then had to catch up. He'd been known to spear two full weeks in one sitting. This week Lenny remembered to shoot a dart each day.

Lenny used a lot of toilet paper that week. He wanted to collect a few more rolls for when Van got back so they could start building their tower. He got out his paints and decorated the rolls with stripes and geometric patterns.

25

Lenny had a dentist appointment for a teeth cleaning with Dr. Selig. Lenny loved having his teeth cleaned because he loved Dr. Selig's instruments: the air pump, the water pick—even the drill as long as it wasn't near his teeth.

"How does this thing work?" Lenny would ask Dr. Selig.

Dr. Selig enjoyed explaining the mechanics of his tools to Lenny. "By pressure, Lenny. This is just like a sandblaster in miniature. Just imagine that I'm sandblasting your teeth."

"I think I might want to be a dentist," Lenny had said to Dr. Selig. "Just so I can use these instruments."

"I'm not sure that's really an adequate reason to become a dentist, Lenny," Dr. Selig had said. "But all power to you."

Lenny had shrugged.

Dr. Selig shoved a wad of cotton into Lenny's mouth. "Are you still thinking about becoming a dentist?" he asked.

"Not sure," said Lenny.

"Having second thoughts?" said Dr. Selig.

Lenny couldn't speak very well with his mouth stuffed with cotton, so he nodded.

"Well, you've got plenty of time to think about it," said Dr. Selig, looking at Lenny's chart. "You're only nine."

Lenny closed his eyes and Dr. Selig began to work. Lenny listened to the hum and buzz of the instruments. He felt the water shoot between his teeth. It tickled. And then the air. The roof of his mouth and his tongue began to feel dry.

"Almost done," said Dr. Selig. When he was finished, he pressed the pump on the chair and Lenny floated back down to earth.

"Does that work by pressure?" asked Lenny, leaning over to examine the chair.

"It sure does," said Dr. Selig.

Lenny's mother was in the waiting room. Lenny smiled, showing her his freshly polished teeth. She smiled back.

"Very nice," she said.

"No cavities," said Lenny.

"I'm happy to hear that," said his mother, hurrying Lenny out to the car.

Lenny's mother whizzed down Belmont Avenue and crossed over onto Pearl Street. Lenny gazed out the window toward Van's house. There was a car in the driveway, and Audrey's stroller was parked out front.

"Hey," said Lenny. "That's Van's parents' car. He must be back already. Can we stop? Please."

Lenny's mother pulled up in front of the house. "Just for a few minutes, Lenny," she said. "Van is probably tired."

Lenny ran up the steps and rang the bell twice. He heard footsteps approaching. The door was opened by Van's father. He was holding Audrey in his arms. Audrey kicked her foot out.

"Hi, Audrey," said Lenny, giving the foot a tickle. Audrey smiled.

"Hi, Mr. James," said Lenny.

"Hello, Lenny," said Mr. James. "Would you like to come in?" Lenny followed him to the kitchen.

"Where's Van?" asked Lenny. "I saw your car. And I guessed you'd be back."

It hadn't registered in Lenny's brain that Mr. James wasn't smiling. In fact, it looked like he had a cold. Or he'd been crying. Van's mother appeared. She looked like she had a cold, too. Suddenly Lenny realized that they'd both been crying.

"Van's gone, Lenny," said Mrs. James. "He didn't survive the operation."

"What do you mean?" said Lenny. "He was supposed

to go to Minneapolis to get fixed. What do you mean he didn't survive the operation?" Lenny's voice was climbing higher, skyward. "What do you mean?" he cried. "He didn't get to build the tower we were planning."

"Vander died," said Mr. James quietly.

"Died like dead?" said Lenny.

"Yes," said Van's mother. "Died like dead."

Lenny's head felt like it was about to explode. He imagined rockets shooting upward, flying to the moon. He imagined gloves raining down over him, all kinds of different-colored gloves. He imagined Van lying there with no hair. He tried to breathe deeply, but it just didn't work. Lenny exploded. He burst into tears.

Lenny felt Mrs. James's arm close around his body.

"I can't stop crying," said Lenny. "This is so awful. Stupid doctors, stupid people. Stupid everyone."

"Don't cry, Lenny," said Mrs. James, rubbing Lenny's back.

"But I want to cry," said Lenny. "I have to cry. Let me cry. I feel sad."

"I know you do," said Mrs. James. "We're all sad. Very sad."

"Hey, Lenny," said Mr. James. He'd put Audrey in her high chair with a cookie. "You know Van really loved you. He talked about you all the time. He said you were the smartest person he ever met. And the nicest."

Mr. James left the kitchen and came back with Van's

robot. "Van asked me to give this to you," he said. "Just in case."

"Just in case what?" said Lenny. "In case he died. You mean Van knew he might die?"

"He did," said Mr. James. "But he would have died for sure without the operation."

Lenny took the robot. Square cakey cheap plastic. No wonder it broke all the time. They really needed to use better materials for these things. Lenny looked at the robot's blank face. Then he felt for the switch on its back. He flicked it and watched the robot's arm lift into the air. It moved slowly from left to right, like it was waving. Then it stopped. It was still broken.

Lenny waved back. "Bye, Van," he said. "Bye, Mr. and Mrs. James. Bye, Audrey." Then Lenny turned with the robot and ran out the door.

Lenny got into the car.

"How is Van?" asked his mother.

"He's resting," whispered Lenny.

"Isn't that his robot?" asked Lenny's mother.

"I'm looking after it for him," said Lenny. "Anyway, it's busted."

" 'Busted' isn't a word, Lenny," said his mother.

"I like to say 'busted,' " said Lenny. "This robot is busted," he repeated. "Busted, busted, busted."

26

When Lenny got home, he went up to his room. He looked at the pile of toilet paper rolls, and the paints that he'd forgotten to put away. Then he took his pillow from his bed. Lenny started to punch. He began around the edges and worked his way to the middle—right to the pit of the pillow's belly. Then he let the pillow fall to the ground. It was misshapen, as if it had had the life beaten out of it. Then Lenny started to cry again.

Lenny heard his mother come in. He felt her standing by his bed.

"Lenny," she said gently. "I've talked to Van's parents. I know about Van, and I'm sorry."

"Don't you cry, too!" shouted Lenny. "We were the only ones left in the world who've never cried. And if you cry, too, then it'll be the end of a species."

Lenny's mother sat down on the bed and hugged him. She handed him a Kleenex with her gloved hands.

"Would you like to take apart the old mixer?" she said. "Maybe you can fix Van's robot."

. . .

"What's wrong, Lenny?" asked Muriel.

"Nothing," said Lenny.

"Lenny, you're wearing a hat and gloves," said Muriel. "It's the middle of May."

"I felt cold today," said Lenny.

"Is there any reason for that?" asked Muriel. "And you've buttoned your shirt wrong."

"Maybe because I'm mad," said Lenny.

"Why?" asked Muriel.

"I don't have any friends anymore," said Lenny.

"What happened to them?" asked Muriel.

"All of my friends, all one of them, died," said Lenny.

Lenny stood up and walked over to his place on the bookshelf. He took off his gloves. Then he took his index finger and flicked the little smiling rubber man off the tower made of blocks.

"I knew we shouldn't have built it so high," said Lenny. "I knew he might fall off and die." Lenny looked at the rubber man, who had rolled to a stop on the floor. It lay there smiling up at him.

"Stop smiling," said Lenny.

"Did something happen to Van?" asked Muriel.

"Van is dead," said Lenny.

"You mean he died?" said Muriel.

"Don't you know what dead means?" said Lenny. "He didn't survive the trip to Minneapolis. He didn't survive the operation."

"Oh, Lenny," said Muriel. "You must be heartbroken."

"I am," said Lenny. "Van was my best friend. He was my only friend."

"I know that," said Muriel. "It's okay to cry, Lenny. It's okay to cry your heart out."

"Then there'll be no one left in the world who's never cried," said Lenny.

"That's okay, too," said Muriel. "Now you can be like all the rest of us."

"Every time I ever love somebody they leave me," said Lenny. "First my father. Then my grandfather. And now Vander James. I really liked him. And he liked me. And now he's dead. Can't you do something, Muriel?" cried Lenny. "Can't you fix my broken heart?"

"I wish I could," said Muriel.

Lenny couldn't stop sobbing. Muriel pulled her chair closer to Lenny and took his hat off. Lenny reached out and took her hand.

"Can I hold your hand, Muriel?" he asked.

"Sure, Lenny," said Muriel. "Hold it as long as you want."

Lenny looked at Muriel's hand. He felt her warm soft

skin, the blood pulsing through her veins to her finger-tips. Her fingernails were smooth. Her thumbnail had a white spot on it.

"You know Lenny, I bet if you asked your mother to take off her gloves so you could really hold her hand, I'm sure she would do it for you," said Muriel.

"No!" shouted Lenny. "I don't want her to take off the gloves."

"But I thought you did, Lenny," said Muriel.

"I don't," said Lenny. "Because if she takes off the gloves, her hands might get old and wrinkled and she might die. What if those gloves are magic? What if she takes them off and she dies?"

"The gloves aren't magic, Lenny," said Muriel. "And your mother's not going to die when she takes off the gloves. I promise you."

"I don't know if I believe you, Muriel."

"You can believe me, Lenny," said Muriel.

27

Lenny took Van's robot to school and into the classroom. He set it on the corner of his desk.

"No toys in the classroom," said Ms. Schillinger. "You know that, Leonard."

"This isn't really a toy," said Lenny.

"No?" said Ms. Schillinger. But she let Lenny leave the robot there. Then she continued diagramming sentences on the board. Lenny loved that, making little road maps of the phrases. Writing the words lopsided at strange angles, dangling from the simple phrase. He waited patiently until Ms. Schillinger paused. Then he raised his hand.

"Do you have something to say, Leonard?" asked Ms. Schillinger. "Make it quick."

"This was Van's robot," said Lenny, holding up the plastic toy. The rest of the class turned and looked at Lenny. Then they looked at the robot. Ms. Schillinger left the phrase she was constructing dangling. She put down her chalk.

"I just want everyone to know that Van is dead," said Lenny. "Officially. You got that? He's officially dead."

"Who's Van?" asked someone.

"Van was my friend," said Lenny.

"What did he die of?" asked someone else.

Lenny looked at Margery. "Leukemia," he said. "That's blood cancer."

Then Lenny looked at the rest of his classmates. Their faces looked thoughtful. It made Lenny feel like crying. But he took a deep breath and let it out. He did this a couple of times. Then he pushed the switch on the back of the robot. He'd repaired it with parts from his mother's old mixer. The robot began waving. This time it didn't stop.

"Everybody say goodbye to Van," said Lenny. "Please."

The words "Goodbye, Van" spilled out in a staggered chorus of voices.

"Goodbye, Van," Ms. Schillinger said. Then she walked over to Lenny.

"I'm sorry about your friend," she said. "And thank you, Leonard, for sharing that with us and letting us say goodbye."

Lenny turned off the robot and set it back on the corner of his desk.

28

Lenny climbed onto his bed. He reached up and pulled out the tacks that held his starship poster to the wall. The *Enterprise*. Lenny rolled it up and snapped a rubber band around its middle. Then he got the dragon that Van had made for him: the dragon that kept away evil and represented all that was good. He tacked it up in the square shadow where the starship had been and he looked at it for a long time. There was a lot of green. Van had liked the color green. Just like Lenny. Just like Muriel.

Lenny went downstairs and flipped on the television. It was time for Dexter. Dexter was mixing a potion to make things invisible.

Lenny's mother came into the living room and sat down next to him.

"What are you watching?" she asked.

"Dexter," said Lenny. "He's a scientist. But he's just a kid."

"What's he doing?" asked Lenny's mother.

"He's trying to make things invisible," said Lenny.

His mother nodded.

Lenny looked down at her hands resting in her lap. She was wearing light blue gloves. They matched her blouse. Lenny lifted up one of her hands.

"I wish you'd take this glove off," said Lenny. "Just for a few seconds."

Lenny's mother looked puzzled. But she slipped off the glove. Then she reached over for Lenny's hand. Her hand was warm and soft. Lenny was afraid of squeezing it too hard, but he didn't let go of it. Not until Dexter had drunk the potion and disappeared from the screen.

"I wish you didn't have to wear those gloves all the time," said Lenny.

"I know," said Lenny's mother. "But it's part of my job."

"You could take them off when you're watching TV," said Lenny.

"I could," said his mother.

"But you don't watch TV very much," said Lenny. He picked up the remote control and switched the channel. It was 4:20. Time for the ad for Plus dishwashing liquid. Lenny watched the hand appear like a phantom on the screen.

"You know," said his mother, "that hand on TV isn't

real. This is real," she said, letting go of Lenny's hand and holding hers up for him to see.

It was like the hand on TV. But Lenny noticed that the skin was slightly darker. And you could see the veins and a very small wrinkle at the wrist. Lenny was glad.

"Maybe you could watch TV a little more often," said Lenny.

"I can try," said his mother. She reached for Lenny's hand and squeezed it tight.

Lenny flipped the channel and Dexter reappeared on the screen. His magic potion had worn off.

The next day, Bob came over. It was Saturday. He was wearing sneakers and his Reds T-shirt.

"I thought we might shoot a few hoops," he said to Lenny.

"I'm pretty busy," said Lenny.

Bob's face fell.

"I was actually wanting to ask you a favor," said Lenny.

"Sure," said Bob. "Anything I can do to help."

"I need some Plexiglas," said Lenny.

"What for?" asked Bob.

"I need to cover something," said Lenny. "It needs to be waterproof and airtight."

"Just tell me what you need to cover," said Bob.

Lenny took Bob to his room and showed him the toilet paper tower. It had taken seven days to build. And it was three feet high and one and a half feet wide.

"One hundred and eighty-one toilet paper rolls in all," said Lenny. "Ten modules. I want to put it up in the playground. Near the slide. But I don't want it to get wet or anything. Or the wind to blow it over. It's kind of fragile."

"I can imagine," said Bob. He walked around the tower. "This is pretty amazing, Lenny," he said. "Can I touch it?"

"If you're careful," said Lenny.

"Oh, I will be," said Bob. He ran his hand along the toilet paper rolls, stiff with dried paint. "It's very impressive," he said. "Did you do it all by yourself?"

"I had some help at the beginning, with the painting," said Lenny. "But then the guy who was doing it died."

"You mean your friend, Van," said Bob. "Your mother told me about that." Bob cleared his throat.

"He liked to build towers," said Lenny. "Just like me."

"I know," said Bob. "I'd like to help if I can."

"Do you think you could get me some Plexiglas to cover this?" asked Lenny.

"I'll be happy to," said Bob. "We'll have to take the measurements. And we'll need some sealant for the joints."

Lenny got a tape measure and held it up to the tower. He called out the figures, and Bob took them down on a small notepad that he pulled from his pants pocket.

"It'll take a few days," said Bob. "Is that all right?"

"Sure," said Lenny.

29

Bob brought over the Plexiglas pieces a few days later—a base, and five other panels, which he and Lenny put together in the driveway and sealed. Lenny went to his room and got the modules. Then he began to reassemble them on the Plexiglas base.

"I think we'd better anchor it," said Bob. "I've got some clear silicone."

"Good," said Lenny.

Lenny pointed out the rolls that Van had painted. They were connected to his. That made Lenny feel good. Many of them were colored like a rainbow. When Lenny was finished, he and Bob put the Plexiglas frame over the tower. Lenny had written a small message on a piece of cardboard, which he'd taped to the inside of the Plexiglas: *For my friend, Van.* Then he signed his name: *Lenny.*

"Would you like me to take you over to the playground with it?" asked Bob. Bob had a van. "I'd be happy to."

"Okay," said Lenny.

"Then maybe we can shoot some hoops," said Bob.

"Okay," said Lenny a second time.

Lenny stood beside the tower at recess. Children passed by and stopped to look. Lenny waited for someone to knock it over. But no one did. Some of them asked, "Who's Van?"

"My friend," answered Lenny.

Others asked, "Did you make that?"

"Van helped," said Lenny.

No one made fun of the tower. For Lenny it was like no one making fun of him.

Will wanted to know how many toilet paper rolls they'd used.

"One hundred and eighty-one," said Lenny.

"That's a lot," said Will.

"It could have been a lot more," said Lenny.

• • •

"What's that, Lenny?" asked Muriel.

"It's Van's robot," said Lenny. "I fixed it for him, even though he's not here. He gave it to me when he died."

"I bet it makes you feel good to have it," said Muriel.

"Yup," said Lenny. "If I die, I'd like you to look after my tower."

"The one on the playground?" asked Muriel.

"Did you see it?" asked Lenny.

"I did, and I think it's beautiful," said Muriel.

"That's Plexiglas on the outside," said Lenny. "They wouldn't have allowed real glass on the playground. Someone might have fallen on top of it and cut an artery or something."

"That would have been tragic," said Muriel. "I think the Plexiglas was a perfect solution."

"Bob got it for me," said Lenny.

"That was nice of him," said Muriel. "I guess you're getting to know Bob a little better."

"A little," said Lenny.

"Getting to know people isn't always easy," said Muriel. "But I think you've made a good start. I'm proud of you, Lenny."

"I'm proud of me, too," said Lenny.

Lenny got up and walked over to his space. He looked at the objects placed carefully on the shelf. Muriel had left the blocks where they'd fallen. But she'd picked up the rubber man, bent him at the waist, and set him on the edge of the shelf. Lenny stacked the tumbled blocks again, one upon the other. Then he made a circle with the other objects around the tower—the clown, the marble, the rubber man, the jumping bean, the basketball, and the acorn. Lenny picked up the acorn and held it in his hand.

"Could I have this acorn?" he asked Muriel.

"Sure," said Muriel.

"It reminds me of Van with the little hat and the smiling face," said Lenny. "Do you think if I planted it, a tree might grow?"

"I don't know, Lenny," said Muriel. "But you can try."

"Van didn't grow into a big tree," said Lenny.

"No, he didn't," said Muriel. "As we said, not all acorns grow into big trees."

"Van got buried, but I don't think another person is going to grow where he's buried," said Lenny.

"I don't think so either," said Muriel. "You probably wouldn't want another person to grow there."

"Nope," said Lenny.

"You know, Lenny, even though Van's dead you don't have to forget about him," said Muriel. "People continue to live on in our minds and hearts and in things we've done with them and for them. Like your tower."

"I'm always going to remember Van," said Lenny.

"I know you are," said Muriel. "I am, too. And I'm always going to remember you, Lenny."

Lenny looked down at his clothes. He was wearing a pair of beige pants and a green shirt. He'd dressed himself without his book of flags. There were no beige flags. Not yet anyway. But someday there might be.

"Are you thinking about anything right now, Muriel?" asked Lenny.

"As a matter of fact I was," said Muriel.

"What?" said Lenny.

"I was thinking about growing up," said Muriel. "How growing up is like waking up. Waking up and seeing something you've never seen before. Seeing the world from a point of view that doesn't start with you. Just between you and me, Lenny, lots of people never grow up."

"I'm not going to be one of those," said Lenny.

"I'm sure you're not," said Muriel. "Is there anything else you'd like to put in your space, Lenny?"

"I'd like to put you in my space," said Lenny. "But you're too big."

"You could put something there that reminds you of me," said Muriel.

"It would have to be something really really nice," said Lenny.

Lenny looked at the shelf of objects. Nothing seemed quite right.

"You don't have to decide today," said Muriel.

Lenny sat back down in his chair. He spun around a couple of times.

"Did that make you feel good?" Muriel asked.

"Yes," said Lenny. "And it gave me a good idea."

"What's that?" asked Muriel.

"Can I use your colored markers?" asked Lenny.

"Sure," said Muriel.

Lenny began to draw a flag on a piece of paper. He

made the background beige like his pants. But then he colored in some green and blue stripes the color of the shirt Muriel was wearing. He cut out the flag and wrapped the edge around a small pencil.

"Would you like some tape?" asked Muriel.

"Yes, thank you," said Lenny.

Lenny attached the flag to the pencil with tape. Then he got up and walked over to his space.

"I think I need some Silly Putty to anchor this flag. Do you have any, Muriel?"

"I do," said Muriel.

Lenny rolled the Silly Putty into a ball. Then he anchored the flag in his space, next to the tower. He took a deep breath and exhaled slowly. The flag fluttered slightly on its pencil post, but the base held firm.

Lenny returned to his chair. He reached deep into his pocket and felt for his acorn.

"That flag is important," said Lenny.

"I know it is," said Muriel.

"It's in my space, but it can be your flag, too, Muriel, if you want it to be."

"I'd like that," said Muriel. "It can be our flag."

"Okay," said Lenny. And he spun around in his chair one last time.